I0788185

Dead Tokyo

Cyberpunk Meets Zombies

TABLE OF CONTENTS

INTRODUCTION

The fog was creeping across the ground, coming in from the dark, unforgiving sea. Lights from the nearby buildings and street lamps pushed desperately against the fog, only managing to light a small circle of the foggy surroundings. The wind was starting to blow gently on this hazy Tokyo shipping port. What a shopping trip this had turned out to be—anything is possible in the year 2066. A dark shadow suddenly dashes between the buildings, pauses, then sprints off to the next building. As the shadow approaches the last building before the long stretch of ground between them and the warehouse that he is desperately hoping is going to be empty, another shadow appears at the back side of the warehouse. The first shadow is an arrogant young man—not at all surprised by the zombie apocalypse starting so suddenly—who looks across the land that is overtaken with wild foliage and starts counting the gates between them and the warehouse.

The shadow that was approaching the back of the warehouse is a young lady fleeing from the zombies that used to be her parents until they tried to eat her. Ashley slides along the back wall of the warehouse, careful to be quiet, pausing to check the windows to ensure that no zombies are hiding out inside. She finally finds a door. Happy to see that it is unlocked, she carefully inches it open, holding her breath as she does.

Squeezing through the door, she pauses to scan as far as possible inside the warehouse. As she enters, she is careful to ensure that the way is clear and slowly makes her way to the front of the warehouse, scouting along the way for anything that she could use as a weapon to protect herself from the zombies. Assuring herself that the warehouse is clear, she clutches the steel pipe that she found, slowly inches upward to sneak a peek out of the front window, and is surprised to see a young man sprinting across and jumping over the fences separating the warehouse from the nearby buildings.

Glancing through the window again to check the young man's progress, making a mental note of the path he was on while spying the door he seemed to be aiming for, she inches her way down the wall, pausing at windows along the way to check his progress whenever possible. Reaching the door, she glides her hand across the wall until she finally locates a light switch. She flicks the switch, breathing a sigh of relief that the lights still work.

With no window close enough for her to look out, she pauses for an instant, taking in a deep breath and calling on every ounce of reserve she has left.

She simultaneously turns on the lights and opens the door. The light spills out the door and the nearby windows—as the approaching young man skids to a halt at the edge of the circle of light. Ashley watches as he runs his eyes over her from head to toe. Giving a slight shake of his head and painting his face with a cocky smirk, he saunters up to the door, expecting her to move out of the way.

As he approaches and attempts to brush by, Ashley widens her stance and braces her legs and tightens her grip on the pipe she holds in her hands. Surprise shows in his eyes as he eases to a halt mere inches from her. Ashley scans the overgrowth surrounding the warehouse, ensuring that no zombies are approaching.

"Come on in—but one wrong move, and it'll be your last," the woman says to the young man as she turns and steps through the open doorway.

Stepping in behind her, he pulls the door shut behind him and slides the bolt. Let's just ease off on the psycho talk, babe," he says to Ashley.

She raises her eyebrows, and the smug look on his face slips. "My name is Ashley," she says, "and you would be?"

"My name is Chad. It's nice to meet you, Ashley," he replies.

"How did you come to be here?" he asks.

"I had some zombies chasing me, and when I got away, I headed out of town trying to get away from where most of them would likely be," Ashley answers.

"I've been working this way for a while—trying to avoid the zombies and trying to find a weapon at the same time," Chad says.

"I need to finish making sure all the exits are secured," Ashley says to Chad before turning and disappearing inside the warehouse. She eases her way through the warehouse, checking all the doors and scanning out each window. Reaching the door where she had entered, she double-checks the lock and then glances out the window and sees another young man creeping up on the warehouse.

"From the look on his face, he'd probably jump out of his skin if I jumped out and yelled boo," she says to herself. "I don't think this one is any threat," she thinks as she slides the bolt on the door. Opening the door, she steps into the doorway and sees the fear jump into his eyes as he comes to an instant halt.

"Hi, I'm Ashley. You're welcome to come in if you want," she says to him. After a nervous look around, the young man comes to the door, and she steps aside to let him pass.

Once inside the warehouse, Ashley turns and locks the door. He blurts out, "My name is Brad." After a nervous look around, Brad says, "How long have you been here?"

"I just came here a couple of hours ago," Ashley responds. "There is another young man here named Chad," she says to him. "He shortly arrived after I did." Turning and waving her arm for Brad to follow, Ashley heads back to where she had last seen Chad. Once Chad is in sight, she says, "I found another stray creeping around out back." Brad's cheeks turn bright pink, and he seems to sink into himself. "Chad, this is Brad. Brad, this is Chad," she says and then spots the pipe that Chad has found somewhere.

"Welcome, Brad. How did you come to be here, and where did you come from?" Chad says and then locks his eyes on Brad, waiting for a response.

Licking his lips and glancing nervously back and forth between Chad and Ashley, Brad finally speaks, "I was in the downtown area when people started turning to zombies, I locked the door and stayed very quiet until I realized that I couldn't stay there anymore." He shivers and continues, "I am not a particularly brave person, as I am more of an electronics geek. I was so scared heading out to come here, and that's why it took me days to get this far."

"I had zombies chasing me. I figured that there would be less of them this far out, so that's why I came here," Ashley says.

Then, Chad speaks up, "I worked my way here searching for

food and a weapon. We need to kill them all." Brad and Ashley turn to look at Chad in unison.

"I need to recheck the outside," Ashley says as she turns and heads to the front of the warehouse. Looking out the window, she spots another young man making his way to the warehouse. She stands there and watches for a few minutes. "Interesting," she says, "he's not creeping or sauntering, but it's kind of a stroll," she muses to herself.

Feeling the fluttering sensation in her chest and a brief tingle in her breasts, she realizes that there is an attraction there. Squinting and cocking her head slightly to one side, she watches for a couple more minutes. "I wonder how that happened," she thinks. She heads towards the door and sliding back the lock opens it and steps into the doorway—and leaning seductively against the door frame, she pastes a welcoming smile on her face.

The approaching young man doesn't even break stride but returns the smile. As he approaches, he holds out his hand and says, "Hi, my name is James."

Placing her hand in his, Ashley says, "Hi, I'm Ashley. It is nice to meet you. There are two more guys inside—Chad and Brad. Chad got here just after me, and Brad just showed up half an hour ago." Then, out of nowhere, she continues, "My parent's skin exploded, and they turned into sore filled zombies, and then they tried to eat me. I ran, and I managed to escape—I couldn't bring myself to hurt them even if I know that they are no longer my parents, but I got away—and then I came here."

Hearing her story, James sympathetically pulls her into a gentle hug.

Ashley melts against him, shuddering out a sigh—she hasn't felt this safe since her parent's skin started exploding. Easing back, Ashley looks up into James' eyes and quietly whispers, "Thank you. I didn't realize how bad I needed that."

James lowers his arms and says, "You're quite welcome. That is a terrible thing for anyone to have had to go through. You are an amazingly strong woman." He turns and looks out over the surrounding area. With a wistful look on his face, he says, "I wish we could go to a place where there are no zombies—but they're everywhere. I just want to go somewhere where it's beautiful and peaceful."

Ashley looks at James and reaches for his hand and says, "Come on, I'll go and introduce you to the other two." Leading James through the door, she releases his hand and turns to secure the door. Upon finding Chad and Brad looking at a couple of human-shaped robots, she says, "James, this is Chad," nodding in Chad's direction, "and this is Brad."

Chad turns to James and extends his hand and says, "Welcome to our little group. I'm Chad, and I'm the leader. We are—"

Ashley steps in and slaps his hand down and says, "I don't know who the hell you think you are, but you are not the leader of anything. I was here before you."

Brad seems to disappear into himself again, and James looks back and forth between Ashley and Chad. "I think we can all work together without having a leader. Has anyone checked out the warehouse to see what we have to work with? We're going to have to find some food."

Chad re-extends his hand and says, "Welcome to the group." James shakes his hand and says simply, "Thank you."

Brad says, "Hey, James, nice to meet you," and James steps over to Brad. Shaking his hand, he says, "Thank you, Brad. It's nice to meet you, too!"

Ashley then says, "As I told you outside, I came here because some zombies were chasing me and trying to eat me. Chad went this way searching for a weapon of some sort because he has the misguided notion that we should try to kill them all and take the city back."

Meanwhile, Brad speaks up and repeats his story of hiding in his apartment trying to work up the nerve to try and escape to somewhere safe.

James then says, "I came this way looking for somewhere to find food and dreaming of a place that's beautiful and zombie-free."

Chad scowls his face and says, "There is no getting to somewhere like that. This is a zombie apocalypse, and the world as we knew it is over. You might as well get used to that. The only way is to kill them all."

James says, "I think you just like the thought of all this killing with somewhat an acceptable reason. Don't you think there are better ways than fighting and killing?"

"Think what you want, but they're not going away on their own," Chad quips.

"I think the first thing we should concentrate on," says Ashley, "is to check out the warehouse and see what resources we might have available to us. Brad, why don't you go with Chad and head that way," she motions with her arm to the area of the warehouse behind Chad, "and I'll go with James and go this way? Then, we'll meet back here and see what we've got."

Ashley turns and heads down the hallway, while Chad and Brad head the opposite direction. James hurries to catch up to Ashley, and she turns and smiles warmly at him. As they walk and investigate, they talk about survival, and Ashley tries to steer the conversation to thoughts of what the future might hold.

CHAPTER 1

As Chad heads down the hallway, with Brad trailing along behind, he thinks to himself that if that dreamer James and the messed-up broad get Brad to join their ranks, they'll have all the power. He decides that it would be worthwhile to ensure Brad's loyalty to him and at least keep the power as balanced as possible. With such a goal in mind, he turns to Brad and says, "Let's check every room we come to and leave no area unchecked. We want to find the most resources so that the other two can't claim to be in charge because they found more."

Brad blinks and smiles at Chad and says, "Yeah, let's show them," even as he thinks that they didn't seem to be trying to take charge. Chad was the strong one, in his eyes, because he didn't want to sit back and do nothing. He had all the courage that Brad wished he possessed but was honest enough with himself to admit that he didn't.

As Ashley and James explore their end of the warehouse, Ashley continuously steals glances at James, who is quite enjoying the smile that plays at her lips every time her eyes land on him. They talk as they search all the rooms and different sections of the building. There is a comradery between them that makes it seem to Ashley that she has known James forever—even if she has never laid eyes on him before today.

Ashley tears her eyes from James and opens the door on her right. As she steps through the door, she flips the light switch. "Holy shit," she exclaims.

James comes to the door and says, "What did you find?"

She points to the two robots standing in the corner of the room and then motions to the bodysuits complete with VR headsets hanging on the wall.

"Holy shit is right," says James as he quickly walks over to examine the robots. "We should check them out and see if they work."

They switch on the robots and find out that they are charged up. They quickly suit up, and Ashley grins, looks at James before slipping the VR helmet on, and says, "Let's use them to go see what Chad and Brad are up to."

With a chuckle, James agrees before pulling his own VR helmet onto his head. Suited up, they begin maneuvering the robots to the other end of the warehouse to see what Chad and Brad are doing.

Chad and Brad are checking out a room full of items, and Brad exclaims, "Look at all these tools and equipment! If we could find the right materials, we can build all kinds of things."

As Ashley and James control the robots, they hear Brad's exclamation and turn and head in that direction. As the robots step into the doorway, Brad practically jumps behind Chad.

Chad looks over the robots and says, "Nice, we could sure make use of these."

The robots wave their arms for Brad and Chad to follow them and turn and head back to where the group had split up in the center of the warehouse. When they get to the main area, Ashley and James remove the suits and hurriedly head to the meeting area.

As they come into the main area, Chad turns to look at them and smiles as he says, "Nice find, you two. We found a room full of tools and equipment, so with the proper materials, we can make lots of things to help us out."

"Did you finish exploring your end of the warehouse?" James asks Chad.

"I think there were one or two rooms that we didn't get to yet" Chad replies.

"Well, then let's finish our search and meet back here," James says.

Ashley falls into step beside James as they head back to where they found the robots. Brad and Chad head back to where they had been when the robots showed up. After finishing their searches, they meet in the central area. Ashley and James report that they found some unfinished robots and the suits to control them.

Chad comes in with Brad following him, carrying something with a screen on it. James and Ashley look at him as he explains that it is a live feed that can be linked to the robots so that someone other than the robot operators can have a broader view and could help with directions if needed to escape the zombies.

"We also found enough supplies that we can use to repair and or build robots," says Brad.

"That's awesome," says Ashley. "We should be able to use the robots to go out and find food, and that way, we would be less at risk from the zombies," she then suggests.

"That's a good idea," says Chad.

"We should probably wait till it's daylight out, though," says James. "I mean—we don't have night vision on these robots."

"We don't have—that's true," says Brad, "but I've seen these robots before, and they can run super-fast, jump super high, and climb buildings—not to mention that they have enormous strength. With the camera that is mounted here, the user sees through the robot in the first-person view."

"Ok, so let's get some sleep, and we'll plan it out and go find some food tomorrow when it's daylight," Ashley says before turning and heading towards a room to the left of the main area. James follows her with his eyes. Ashley then turns toward him and says, "You're welcome to bunk in here with me if you want to."

"Thanks," says James and turns to follow Ashley into the room.

Brad and Chad move to a room at the back of the warehouse on the opposite side of the main area. "Do you really think we'll be able to find food tomorrow?" Brad asks Chad.

With a cocky grin on his face and a twinkle in his eye, Chad turns to Brad and says, "Don't worry, my friend. I'll get us some food tomorrow and kill a bunch of zombies at the same time."

Everyone settles in for the night and has the best sleep they've had in weeks, feeling more secure with others around to help protect each other.

Early the next morning after the best sleep she had in weeks, Ashley climbs out of her makeshift bed. She takes a quick glance across the room to where James is sleeping, and with a smile on her face, she heads out to the main area just as Chad emerges from his room.

"Good morning, beautiful," Chad says with a sardonic smile.

Ashley just looks at him and then says, "Good morning, Chad."

Moments later, James exits his room, and Brad comes out of his space almost simultaneously. Brad sees Chad and visibly relaxes, then greets the whole group.

James, Ashley, and Chad all echo the greeting, and then they gather to discuss the plans for the mission to find food.

"I can set up the live feed if whoever isn't in one of the robots can monitor it and help the ones in the robots by telling them what they need to do and maybe give directions if they need it," says Brad.

Impressed that Brad has spoken up considering how timid he is, Ashley volunteers to man the live feed while Brad and James run the robots.

"We should go to the McDonald's. They're bound to have some burgers in their freezer," says James.

"Did you ever think maybe some of us want something besides burgers?" says Chad.

"Easy, boys. We're on the same team, remember?" says Ashley.

"We could check for other sources of food on the way there, and if we don't find any, we could go to McDonald's for this time," Brad whimpers in a pleading voice.

"I think we should come up with a weapon for the robots so that they can fend off the zombies when they encounter them," Ashley says.

"I can attach some of those metal rods that Brad and Chad

found yesterday," says James.

"I'll attach my own to my robot; I don't need it falling off when I'm trying to kill a zombie," retorts Chad.

"Remember, we're on the same team," reminds Ashley.

Brad sets about setting up the live feed for Ashley to monitor and then sets up the equipment that he needs to control the robots' radio frequency. James and Chad finish attaching their metal rods to their robots and then suit up. Brad runs some checks to ensure that the guys controlling the robots can see in the first person as well as making sure that the live feed is working accurately.

James and Chad suit up and get comfortable with the robots. Ashley opens the door for them, and they exit the warehouse and begin the journey towards the downtown section where the McDonald's is located. Their super-fast running ability allows them to make good time to the outskirts of the downtown area.

James slows down to a walk and starts looking left and right, trying to spot both zombies and anywhere that might have some food for them. Chad looks back to scc where James went and says, "What the hell are you doing?"

"I'm watching out for zombies and looking for somewhere that we might get something more than burgers. Isn't that what you said you wanted?" retorts James.

"We should just make some noise as we go and draw out the zombies and kill them," Chad says.

"You might want to consider that all we have for weapons are these metal rods," James says, moving the arm with the metal rod attached to it. Then, he continues, "If you draw too many of them, they're going to kill the robots, and then we'll have nothing."

"Come on, guys let's work together—we all need food to survive. We're supposed to be working as a team," Ashley reminds them.

"Don't worry, Chad, we can kill any zombies that try and stop us," says James. James stops his robot for a minute and turns to look at Chad, "We may not like each other much, Chad—but when we're out here, we are here as part of the group. We need to have each other's backs."

"Agreed. Our fights won't interfere in our working together on the missions," Chad replies.

They resume their journey towards the McDonalds, and Ashley tells them that so far, all is clear. They check out a couple of restaurants on the way by, but all the food has already been cleaned out. Thus, they continue to the McDonald's restaurant. Ashley, monitoring the live feed, can steer them around a smaller group of zombies, but she also gets to watch another lone male who isn't so lucky.

The zombies descend in a frenzy on the individual and rip him apart. First, they rip off his arms, and by that time, he's on the ground without hope. Then, one of his legs is pulled off. Ashley wants to turn away, but she just can't tear her eyes from the grisly sight.

At her first gasp, James and Chad pause and ask in unison, "What's wrong?"

She tells them what she just saw, and as she sees them come on screen not too far away, she steers them around the scene. Figuring there's nothing they can do for the guy being eaten, there's no point in exposing themselves any sooner than necessary.

They continue on and soon are standing outside the McDonalds restaurant. They cautiously enter the restaurant and search for any zombies that may be around. Finding the way clear, they make their way slowly down the stairs heading for where the freezer would be. "There it is," Chad exclaims, motioning with his arm to a freezer standing in the corner.

They walk over to the freezer and discover that it is locked. Chad begins looking around for something to help open the freezer and James bends down to look closer at the lock. "Your robots are super strong; just use them to pull it open," Brad insists. Chad joins James, and together, they grip the freezer door and are able to pull it open.

It opens with a loud screech and the sound of metal tearing. "Better check for zombies," says Chad. He turns and heads back towards the stairs as James reaches into the freezer. Grabbing the frozen burgers and fries, James hears Chad battling some zombies. He finishes collecting the rest of the burgers and turns to help Chad with the zombies as much as he can with his arms full.

Maneuvering the burgers and fries to one side, James is able to swing his left arm but only a short distance that may slow down but certainly won't kill any of them.

"We could really use guns for this shit," says Chad.

"I know" is James' frantic reply. "I think, once we're outside, we'll have to use our robots' super-fast speed. I can't jump and climb a building with my arms full."

Chad continues to battle the zombies with his metal rod and

discovers that if he hits at just the right angle, he can actually knock the zombies' heads off. As he walks through the slippery gore fighting for the exit, James is close behind helping as much as he can.

As they break through and out into the gray day, Chad says, "We'll have to go right and circle back."

James and Chad grunt in reply and turn to the right and engage the super-fast running ability of their robots. James looks back over his shoulder to see hordes of zombies descending on the McDonalds.

Once they outdistance the masses of rotting, walking bodies, they turn north for a couple of blocks before swinging east to head back to the warehouse. With Ashley guiding them via the live feed, they make it to the warehouse without encountering any more zombies. As they approach, Ashley moves to the door and opens it, allowing the robots inside and then securing the door once again.

When they are in and settled, the food is set down, the robots are turned off, and James and Chad exit the control suits. Both are soaked with sweat and head off to the shower room they located during their search.

CHAPTER 2

While Chad and James are in the shower, Ashley takes the food to the little kitchen area that she and James had found during their search. She assumes that it must have been the break room for the employees before this damn zombie outbreak. Brad, meanwhile, checks out the robots for any visible damage and plugs them in to recharge. "I'll have to get a report from Chad and James later on their performance," he thinks to himself.

Ashley can hear Chad and James arguing over killing all the zombies or leaving for somewhere with more survivors before she can see them coming down the hall. Heaving a sigh, she braces herself for yet another round of playing referee. Brad is listening intently to what they're saying with a pensive look on his face.

Ashley, studying Brad, gets the sense that he will side with Chad whether he agrees with him or not. "It's like Chad is his idol and as he worships him," she thinks to herself. Realizing that means they have selected sides, so to speak, she decides that she should share these realizations with James.

"If we killed all the zombies, we could come and go as we please without any worry anymore," Chad says, trying to get James to see his point of view.

"If we went somewhere with more survivors and fewer zombies, it would be easier to protect and kill all the zombies. Then, we could start rebuilding the human race and get back to normal," retorts James.

Chad tries his best to steel his features into an unreadable mask and thinks that if he doesn't want to fight the zombies, why doesn't he just admit it instead of trying to pretend he wants to go somewhere else to make things better. "I think I'll have to work harder on making sure Brad is going to take my side in this," he decides. "Do you have any idea how hard it would be to leave here and go somewhere else?" he asks.

James pauses to think about it, then replies, "It may not be easy, but that doesn't mean that we should give up."

"We don't even have a ship," Chad retorts. "What are you going to do—swim somewhere else?"

James can't believe how determined Chad is to stay in a city so overrun with zombies that the only hope they have of survival rests with the robots that they have found. James is glad to see that they are approaching the main area and hopes one of the other two are there so that they can take a break from this argument.

"I think we can all agree that we would like to have a life with no zombies," Ashley says as Chad and James come into the main area from the hallway.

"That doesn't mean staying and fighting the huge number of zombies that are here with only us four is the right answer," Chad interjects. "If we go somewhere else, even if it were miraculously possible, we wouldn't have any robots to help us because we'd have no way to recharge their batteries."

"Maybe we could find a generator or two," James suggests, "then we would have the ability to take our robots with us and be able to recharge their batteries."

Seeing the disagreement in Chad's eyes even though his face

remains like stone, James decides to try a different train of thought.

"You do realize that we don't have an endless supply of food, and our supply of machine parts is not huge," James begins, when Chad jumps in with:

"But if we kill the zombies, we can scour the whole city without the robots."

"I think it would be great if there were no zombies, Chad. I'm just not sure that staying here and fighting them is better than going somewhere with more people and fewer zombies to fight," continues James.

"I think James is right, and it makes logical sense to have more people and fewer zombies," Ashley thinks to herself. "I don't understand why he is so determined to stay here and kill the zombies. Why would it matter if we kill the zombies here or somewhere else as long as we get rid of them—so we can live safely?"

"While we're here, I think we should work together to make our position as secure as possible—and then we can look at ways to be able to go somewhere else," Ashley says, sending James a hopeful look.

"We are stronger when we're together," James admits.

"I think Chad has a point, though," says Brad, looking wistfully at his newfound hero. "I'm on his side in this—I say we kill all those zombies and get the city back."

"Well, I, for one, am declaring war on those fucking zombies," says Chad and stands and stomps from the room.

"I'm with him," says Brad, who then races off after Chad.

Ashley looks at James, who rolls his eyes and shrugs his shoulders. Ashley bursts out giggling, "That about sums it up," she says.

"I don't know why he is so determined to kill all the zombies here," Ashley says to James. "Does it really matter whether we kill them all here or somewhere else—as long as we can live peacefully without zombies?" she continues.

"I think he is afraid of change, and that's why he won't even listen to reason about going somewhere with fewer zombies," James says. "I wouldn't want him to be in charge of planning any missions for me," James says, shaking his head. "He doesn't think of the possible repercussions of his actions. He wants to go start killing zombies—doesn't he realize that the rest of them will chase him?" he says.

"I know what you mean," replies Ashley. "Personally, I would much rather go somewhere else with you where there are more people and fewer zombies."

James turns his head, furrowing his brow, as he looks at Ashley. "Thanks for the vote of confidence," he smiles, "but he did have some points when he said that without a ship, and with limited food, it is going to be hard to go somewhere else."

"That doesn't mean we shouldn't try. I can see your dream of being somewhere beautiful—with more people for protection and maybe with fewer zombies that could be killed more easily. We could get to know each other better and—" Ashley leaves the sentence unfinished, as her cheeks turn pink.

James notices the pink creeping up into Ashley's cheeks and can't help thinking that she sure is beautiful when she's blushing. Then, the thought occurs to him that maybe she is thinking similar thoughts about him. He lets his thoughts drift over her last statement, wondering if there is any hidden meaning in there.

Chad and Brad had walked to the far end of the warehouse where they had found the pile of supplies. Chad looks at Brad and says, "Thanks for the support. I thought I might be becoming a lone wolf back there."

"You're strong and sure of yourself," Brad replies. "I would rather stake my survival on you than a dreamer and a woman."

Chad, deciding that this is a good time to ensure Brad stays on his side, says, "I think Ashley is smart even if she is a woman, but I don't think we can convince her to switch sides." Sensing the loyalty in Brad, he decides to continue, "We need to stick together. We'll work with them on missions to provide for our survival, but when it comes to leaving, they're on their own."

"It's too bad that we don't have any explosives here," Chad says with a chuckle.

"We could send them out with a bang," Brad agrees. "I think we should go to the gun store and get some guns and ammunition," declares Chad. "I could search for some kind of explosives while I'm there," he says.

Chad falls silent and stares at the pile of materials laying on the floor. "What's the matter?" Brad asks. However, Chad is lost in thought—and if he hears him, he doesn't answer.

Brad stands stock, still glancing nervously at Chad. Finally, Chad turns and says, "Can you make some sort of hidden pocket for my robot?" Brad looks at Chad perplexed.

"Why do you need a hidden pocket?" Brad asks him. "Well I was thinking, when we're at the gun store if I can find some explosives of some kind, James isn't going to agree with me taking them. He doesn't want me to kill all the zombies," Chad says. "Yeah, they'd rather run away and join a bigger group," Brad scoffs.

"I'll see what I can come up with, but I'll have to wait till they're not around to attach it," Brad says. "Thanks" replies Chad. "I could bring my robot back here for you to do some repairs once it's charged," suggests Chad. "What we should do is when they're charged, we can bring them both back here so I can check them over, and then I'll make a hidden compartment for you on yours," suggests Brad.

"I think if we had more people and fewer zombies it would be easier to protect the people, and probably a lot less stressful," James says as he gazes at Ashley noticing the pink in her cheeks. "There might be more to her comment compared to what it seems," he thinks to himself. "We need to rebuild the human race," James says and then as he realizes what he just implied he feels the heat of a blush start up his neck into his cheeks.

Ashley looks at James and the pink in her cheeks blossoms to a red. "How do we keep Chad from starting a war with the zombies?" she asks.

"I'm not sure that we can keep it from happening, but maybe we can slow it down," James muses aloud. "I think we definitely need to get some guns so that we can better protect ourselves and equip our robots for other missions. This food will probably last a week," James says as he looks at Ashley and is surprised to see her looking at him so intently—and as she turns her eyes away, he feels suddenly shy.

"Maybe we should find those other two and start making a plan for getting some guns," Ashley replies. Reaching out tentatively, she takes hold of James' hand. Feeling the surge of warmth and what feels like electricity course through her body, she feels her lips curve into a smile and can almost feel the sparkle in her eye.

James holds her hand for a minute before turning to her and saying, "Why don't we just let them be for now, and we can start working on a plan? We can discuss it with them once they come back."

"Ok, I'll get a map," says Ashley. She reluctantly releases James' hand and walks over to where she had stored the map after planning their last mission. James pulls a couple of chairs up to the table that they have set up in the central area and sits down as Ashley places the map on the table in front of him. Ashley pulls up a chair next to James, and they bend their heads over the document.

"I figure that we probably won't see many zombies between here and here," James says drawing a line on the map with his finger.

"The difficult part will be getting from there to the gun store, which is way over here," Ashley says placing a finger on the location of the store.

"I wonder if we could come up with some sort of a backpack or something so that the robots can carry what we find while still having their arms free for fighting off the zombies that we are sure to encounter," says James.

Coming down the hallway, Chad and Brad catch the last part of the conversation and Chad sarcastically says, "Planning on going out on your own are you?"

"As tempting as that sounds, I think we're stronger as a group," says James.

"We were brainstorming for a mission to get to the gun store and get some firepower," says Ashley—and before Chad can interject as she sees him preparing to do, she continues, "We figured we would brainstorm, and when you two returned, we could all put our heads together to come up with a plan as a team."

Recognizing his chance to complete Chad's secret compartment without suspicion, Brad speaks up, "After the robots are charged I can take them back where the materials are and give them a thorough going over to make sure they're in good operational condition and come up with something to meet your needs."

James has a funny feeling that they're up to something but dismisses it as being suspicious of everything because of the zombies.

Chad and Brad pull up a couple more chairs and look down at the map as the four of them get back to planning their mission to the gun store. They plan out the ideal route they want to take to get to the gun store and back, and knowing the high chance of encountering zombies they choose two alternate routes that they can resort to should circumstances require it.

Ashley leans in to trace out the second of their contingency routes and as she does so her leg rubs up against James'. Her breath catches in her throat as she feels the warmth flow through her. After a moment, she continues, pointing out the different points it would be possible to switch between routes if it was necessary.

"I don't know about this one spot," James says as he leans forward to point out the one spot on the route where they would have no alternative choice and would be boxed in if set upon by zombies. As he does, he is wondering if Ashley would mind if he placed his hand on her leg. Trying to focus on the task at hand he stares at the map looking for an alternative and doesn't realize when his hand, of its own accord, comes to rest on the back of Ashley's leg that is pressing up against him.

By the time he realizes it's there, he is already sliding his hand up and down her leg. Pulling his hand away he looks up to see Ashley smiling at him. "What about this route?" Ashley says drawing a new line on the map with a pencil they had found.

"That could work, there's nowhere to be cut off from an escape route," puts in Chad.

"Alright, why don't you and Chad move the robots to the work area," Ashley says to James, "and while you do, I'll cook us up some of those burgers and fries."

They store the map away and head off to do their separate tasks, each lost in their thoughts.

CHAPTER 3

As Ashley makes her way to the kitchen area, she thinks how normal this could seem without the zombies and the constant threat of death that they present. A blush warms her cheeks as she contemplates James while setting about her task of preparing some of the burger patties and fries that they took from McDonald's. With the patties sizzling and the chips in the oven, she lets her mind wander.

Chad and James get suited up and move the robots to the work area so that Brad can give them their check-up and come up with a way for them to carry the guns and ammo that they hope to find. After removing the suits, Chad says, "I'm going to go give Brad a hand, at least as much as I can." He saunters off down the hallway.

James looks after him and thinks about following then decides against it and instead turns to head to the kitchen where Ashley is preparing their lunch. "I thought I would come to see if I could be of any assistance," James says as he comes into the kitchen area and sees Ashley standing near the stove looking lost in thought like she's a thousand miles away.

Ashley turns and smiles at him as the blush creeps up her cheeks. Glad he can't read her mind, she freezes as James smilingly says, "A penny for your thoughts."

She blushes deeper as she looks over what she was thinking. Not wanting to lie to him, she turns and looks at him and licking her lips says, "I was thinking about what it would be like to be with you where there are no zombies—this would almost be normal cooking for you and your friends.”

James looks at her, blinks his eyes twice, and cocks his head to one side—and then all of a sudden, his eyes light up like a light bulb just went on, and he smiles. “You mean, like you and me together as in dating, right?”

Ashley nods as she can’t seem to find her voice. James approaches Ashley, and as she turns towards him, he wraps his arms around her waist and lowers his lips to hers. Her arms automatically go around his neck, and she increases the pressure of the kiss.

After a moment, James eases back, and she looks up into his eyes and says,” You can help me carry the food out to the table if you want,” before planting a quick kiss on his lips and turning back to the stove. James spies the hot mitts sitting on the counter and picking them up and slipping his hands inside heads to the oven to retrieve the fries.

Ashley and James place the food on the table, and Ashley heads back to the kitchen to get some plates and cutlery. James walks down the hall to tell Chad and Brad that lunch is ready. They all meet at the table and sit down to have lunch and discuss the plans for the gun store mission.

“To travel that distance with the robots, we’re going to need to take a radio signal extender with us. We’ll need to mount it on a high building,” says Brad.

“You mean I’ll have to mount it to the building,” laughs Chad.

“Well yeah, I’m not going to be there,” Brad replies. “When we’re done with lunch, we’ll have to figure out where the tallest building is and work it into our plan to get there.”

After lunch, Ashley takes the dishes to the kitchen, and James says, "Here, let me help you with those." With the dishes cleaned up, they head back to the table where Chad and Brad are poring over the map.

"I think if we can place the radio signal extender somewhere around here," says Brad, drawing a circle on the map. "The robots should be able just to make it to the gun store, here."

"I think if we sharpen some of these metal rods we can make some spears to take with us until we get to the gun store, it's a more populated area so likely to be many more zombies there," Chad suggests as he gets up and turns toward the hallway.

"I'll give you a hand," says James climbing to his feet and glancing at Ashley as he turns and follows Chad down the hallway.

"I better finish up with the robots," says Brad.

Ashley follows them all down the hallway and reaching the work area, spies Brad closing some sort of door she had never noticed on Chad's robot. Hearing her approach, Brad turns and says, "Hey Ashley, if you look over there on the bench by where the control suits are hanging, I found some bags that they can use to hold the guns and ammo. Could you bring them over so that I can make sure they'll stay on the robots?"

Once they get the bags on, Chad and James get suited up while Ashley helps Brad attach the radio signal extender on the back of James' robot. As they prepare to exit the warehouse, Brad says, "That radio signal extender weighs about a hundred pounds James so you won't be able to jump as high with it on your robots back. You'll have to make use of your speed and run."

James acknowledges this information with a nod and a wave as he and Chad turn and exit the warehouse. Ashley secures the door behind them and moves over to the live feed so she can help guide them to the high-rise where they're going to attach the wireless transmitter. On their way to the high-rise, Chad and James discover that the fastest way to kill the zombies is to chop off their heads.

Becoming proficient at slicing off the zombie's heads, Chad and James dispatch a massive number of zombies on the route to the high-rise. As they approach the building, Ashley has them detour so they can approach the high-rise from the South. "Good thinking, Ashley," says James.

As they near the structure, Chad suggests they climb on the metal part of the building. "It will be stronger to stand the robot hands digging in and holding on," he points out. They begin their climb when a zombie comes crashing through the window reaching out for Chad. James pauses and swings his crude spear at the zombie beheading him in midflight. The zombie falls to the ground—blood and gore splatter against the back of Chad's robot.

In what seems like less than a second, zombies are jumping through all the windows trying to grab them. The breaking glass and loud screeches of the zombies make it sound like a warzone as both Chad and James dodge the flying zombies, slowing down here and a couple of times to take a step down to miss one flying out a window slightly above them.

After what seems an eternity they gain the roof and Chad helps James to get the radio signal extender off his back. They find the best place to mount it, and as they finish attaching the device, the door leading to the roof bursts open and a dozen zombies come pouring out. Chad and James grab their crude spears and turn to face off the zombies.

Chad's first swipe cuts the arm off the zombie that was reaching out for him, and with blood spurting from where it's arm used, to be it continues to advance. His next swipe sends the zombie's head rolling. James is backing toward the edge, and then with a side step, he chops off the head of the zombie closing in on him. The body falls to the roof, blood spurting over the edge of the roof and running down the side of the building as the head rolls off the edge and lands upside down in the bushes below.

Battling his way back towards the transmitter James sends a zombie head rolling across the roof, and the zombie streaking towards Chad stumbles over it and topples off the side of the roof. The crunch when it lands on the ground below is sickening. Chad suddenly jumps towards James spear upraised and James reading the situation, sidesteps as Chad separates the head from the body of the zombie that was attacking from behind.

Finally, when all the zombies that had come pouring out onto the roof are dispatched, they turn their attention back to the wireless signal booster and switch it on. Instantly they can feel the difference in the response of their robots. Now that this part of their mission is complete, they pause for a few minutes and look out over the city.

It looks deserted, with the bright sun glinting off windows, James notes all the bushes and foliage that are growing wildly throughout the city. Looking up, Chad turns to James and says, "The air sure is clear now. Since that cloud that brought the zombie affliction has dissipated, the air is fresher."

James looks up and then looks back over at Chad and replies,

"There are not millions of people polluting the earth now."

"Yeah, it's almost like the earth is reclaiming its land," Chad comments.

With a nod, James agrees and then turns to leave.

Chad and James walk along the edge of the building closest to the gun store and jump down from the roof. They set off in the direction of the store, and suddenly, they notice that everything is getting darker and they hear the screeches that could only come from the zombies. Ashley monitoring from the live feed says, "There are zombies everywhere. If we're going to have any chance at success, you better go up and across the rooftops to avoid them."

With no hesitation at all, James and Chad turn as one and head to the nearest building and jumping up grasp the edge of the roof and pull themselves up. They clamber up and run and jump to the next roof. They pause for an instant and look down, and James exclaims, "Oh my God, look at all the zombies down there."

"If we ever get caught in that mass of walking, rotting flesh, we'll be finished," says Chad.

"Thank God, we're using the robots," says James.

"Yeah, but without them, we'd be in deep shit," Chad reminds him.

With the grim reminder that the swarm of zombies down below spells certain death for anybody that comes into their grasp, they continue their rooftop approach to the gun store. As they land on the roof of the store, James motions Chad over to the middle of the roof and kneels down when they reach it. "These zombies will attack anything they hear that is foreign to them. I think they think it's something they can eat or kill," whispers James.

"We need to find a way in without making any noise, there are thousands of them down there," replies Chad.

As they scan the rooftop looking for easy access, James taps Chad on the shoulder when he spies the rooftop entrance. They quietly make their way over to it, "Remember: no noise, or they'll swarm our robots and kill them, and we'll have nothing to help protect ourselves not to mention no guns or ammunition either," hisses James.

Inspecting the latch on the roof access James comes up with an idea and turning his crude spear around he inserts the thick end beneath the edge of the lap and pulls up. With a quiet ping, the latch lets go. James and Chad both move to the side of the roof and look down to make sure the zombies didn't hear the noise.

Judging it to be safe they move back and silently lift the roof access and James motions Chad to go first. Chad begins down the ladder, and as James comes in, he lowers the roof access back down. As they step off the ladder, they look around and find themselves in a dark room that is eerily silent.

James reaches up and turns on his built-in flashlight which illuminates a counter that is bare except for a cash register. Chad follows suit and switches on his built-in flashlight which illuminates the guns lined up along one wall in racks. "I wonder where the ammo would be," James mutters turning around to look at the other side of the room.

Chad heads over to the guns to fill up his bag, and James

moves off in the opposite direction trying to locate the ammo. Chad fills his bag with a large assortment of guns and then spies something strange looking. Upon moving closer, he grabs an egg-shaped object with a gun-like handle.

Turning it over in his hands he notices the thin pieces of metal coming out from the back and spreading out to leave an inch gap between them and the body of the egg-shaped object at the front. They almost look like talons, Chad thinks to himself and then noticing the dial on the back marked for low and high with notches in between he realizes this is one of the new stunners he had been reading about before the zombie apocalypse began.

Chad stores the stunner in his hidden compartment and as he clicks it shut he hears a loud whoosh and a crash behind him. He turns and sees a zombie on top of James' robot on the floor. Rushing over Chad tries to pry the zombie off James, trying to be quiet in the process.

Finally, after a lengthy struggle, Chad manages to pull the zombie off James, accompanied with a sound of ripping metal and a loud screech from the zombie. Chad wastes no time in grabbing his crude spear and chopping the zombie's head off. Turning back to James, Chad sees a rip in the side of the robot where the zombie has torn the metal loose.

CHAPTER 4

"Is your robot still functioning okay?" Chad asks James.

James climbs to his feet and tries all the functions of his robot and replies, "It seems to be working ok."

"I think that must have been the store owner," James muses.

"Yeah, I just hope the zombies out there didn't hear the noise," Chad mumbles.

All of a sudden, the silence is filled with an earsplitting screeching coming from outside. "I guess they heard," James says as he turns to Chad.

"Hurry up, and grab whatever you can," Chad says as he runs over to a glass cabinet that he had spotted while helping James with the zombie.

Chad grabs all the ammo he can fit in his bag and begins searching for any available explosives. James is frantically stuffing guns in his bag when he spots one of the stunners Chad had found earlier. Glancing surreptitiously over his shoulder, he notices that Chad is focused on the glass case, and he stows the stunner in his bag.

Chad searches through the glass cabinet but finds no explosives. He takes a quick look through the drawer in the bottom of the case and is pleased to uncover a dozen sticks of dynamite and some blasting caps and primer. He tucks them into his secret compartment after glancing at James to make sure he wasn't looking.

As he glances up at the window, Chad sees at least two dozen zombies running toward the store. "We've got to go," he yells as he grabs a few more boxes of ammo from the cabinet.

James, frantically filling his bag with guns, turns to look out the window and says, "Let's get out of here."

They begin making their way to the ladder to get out of the store when a few zombies who have come down the ladder charge at them. Stepping apart, they both swing their crude spears, and each beheads a zombie. Chad gets the third one on his return stroke—the floor is suddenly slick with zombie blood and gore.

They hurry to the ladder, but before they can reach it, ten more zombies come sliding down, cutting off their escape route. Chad veers left, and James dashes right as they begin swinging at the zombies for all they're worth.

Ashley, watching the live feed, sees the zombies swarming towards the gun store and for a few minutes forgets that it is the robots in the store and not actually Chad and James. She is frozen immobile with fear as her heart lodged in her throat at the thought that James may not make it out of the store. It's not until James, in the control suit, stops moving for a moment, that she realizes it's just the robots in the store and James is right here.

Heaving a sigh of relief, she says, "The zombies are closing in on the store, guys; you've got to get out of there."

"We're trying to get out of here," snaps Chad.

"Easy, Chad. I know it's frustrating," pants James, "but you don't need to take it out on her."

"Sure thing, Casanova," Chad retorts. Chad swings his spear and cuts the head off the last remaining zombie and grabs the ladder and hurries up to the roof.

James comes up the ladder a step behind Chad, and they burst out onto the roof in time to see a dozen zombies coming across the roof. "How the hell did they get up here," James wonders out loud.

He spins lashing out with his spear, and before his turn is over, he's chopped off the heads of four zombies. They collapse to the roof spurting blood all over the place. Chad repeats the move on the other side and all the sudden there are only four zombies left.

Chad spots one circling to come up behind James and picks up a zombie's head and uses it like a bowling ball; the zombie trips on it and falls off the roof. James chops the head off of another zombie coming up behind Chad, and Chad turning his head to see, says, "Thanks."

Chad suddenly spins and lunging forward sticks his spear through both heads of the remaining two zombies. James swings his spear and cuts both their heads off in one swing. Chad raises his spear with the two zombie heads impaled on it and says, "Hell yeah."

James helps Chad remove the zombie heads from his spear and then turning they both run across the roof and leap across to the rooftop next door. Turning back, they see zombies pouring into the building from all sides and the top. There are literally hundreds of them climbing over each other trying to get inside, to where they think the men are, so they can kill them and eat them.

They stand on the roof of the building next door, shocked into absolute stillness as the mass of zombies that seems endless pours into the building they have just escaped. They couldn't help but think if they had gotten caught there, it would have resulted in definite obliteration. The robots would be destroyed, and that would have left them unable to obtain food. That would make for a long slow painful death.

Ashley and Brad watch the zombies swarm the building through the view of the cameras on the robots. They are both stunned to silence. And Chad wants to start a war with that, Ashley thinks to herself, what is he thinking? Brad begins to shiver from looking at the mass of zombies still pouring into the gun store.

"Let's get out of here," James urges Chad, and they turn and continue their journey across the rooftops away from the gun store. Once they are out of sight of the zombies, they stop and draw a shaky breath.

Chad turns to James and says, "Holy shit, did you see that? How the hell can we fight that?"

James exhales a slow breath before replying, "I don't think we can. There's four of us and only two robots, and there are thousands of them." Chad stands at the edge of the roof, glaring back in the direction of the gun store. "I realize that you hate them Chad, but it's suicide to try and kill them all," James adds.

"It is with guns," says Chad, "On that point, we can agree—but I'm not going to let them take over this city."

"He's never going to give up until he either wins or dies while trying," James realizes this, and with a sad shake of his head, he turns toward the other side of the building. He stands there surveilling the street below, searching for any zombies that may be in the area. "Are there any zombies around Ashley or are we able to get down and use the street now?" James asks.

"That makes you realize just how perilous our situation is," Chad says as he comes up beside James to stand there scanning for zombies.

"It's difficult to put into words," James replies, "but honestly, without the robots, survival here is hopeless. Winning a war with them is impossible."

"It makes me extremely thankful to have survived and made it to this warehouse," Ashley says softly.

"I can't believe I survived and escaped that," Brad mutters. "I think if I had seen that chasing me I'd probably have just stopped and been eaten."

Ashley turns to look at Brad and says, "You may surprise yourself; you may just put everything you've got into surviving."

"I don't know about you," James says to Chad, "but I'm going to be extra careful on the way back. There's nothing like thousands of zombies pouring into a store to kill and eat you to make you remember that it's deadly out here."

Chad breathes out a sigh and looking at James replies, "There aren't enough words to explain how humbling and humiliating that experience was."

"You should be good to get down off the roof and go whenever you're ready to go," Ashley says.

Chad and James look at each other, and then Chad says, "Well, we might as well get going."

They jump down from the roof and begin running down the road, regularly slowing to check over their shoulders.

As they reach the edge of the built-up area, Ashley says, "Wait a minute!" They both stop instantly and look around but don't see anything. Ashley stares at the live feed looking all around and then announces, "There's a group of zombies coming right toward you one block east of you and two blocks south."

Chad and James look at each other and head west, running as fast as they can. Once they have run four blocks, they turn north and go two more blocks to come to a halt. Ashley surveys the live feed monitoring the progress of the zombies and checking for any others that may be in the area.

"Ok, now they're where you were, and they're heading south. You can head north, but I would go slow and be as quiet as you can be," Ashley says. James and Chad start off heading north, taking every precaution to be as quiet as possible. After they have gone four blocks, Ashley lets out a sigh of relief and says, "All clear; they're gone. You can book it now."

"God, what a day," James chuckles, as he and Chad head off running as fast as possible. Before long, they approach the gates to the warehouse—and as they come through the gates, they ensure that each one is closed securely behind them. When they finally make it to the door of the warehouse, Ashley is standing there waiting for them to come in.

Once the door is locked, they place the bags of weapons and ammo on the table, and Brad speaks up, "Let's take the robots right to the work area so that I can clean them off and check them out. Yours is going to need repairs for sure, James."

James looks at Brad and Chad and says, "I'll be there in a minute. I just need to catch my breath for a minute." Chad shrugs and turns to follow his robot and Brad down the hall to the work area. Once they are out of sight, James says to Ashley, "Once they're out of the way, there's a stunner in that bag that I want you to take and hide somewhere they'll never find it.

Ashley smiles at James and casually says, "Got it."

James turns and follows his robot down the hall, making sure to stay back a few meters. As his robot approaches the corner, he slows down and positions the camera to see around the corner and watches as Chad pulls out the dynamite, caps, and primer. Then he audibly gasps as Chad pulls the identical stunner out of the compartment on his robot as he just sent Ashley to hide.

James backs his robot up a few feet from the corner and then starts making noise as he walks so he won't seem to be spying. He brings his robot up beside Chads' and steps out of the suit. Hanging the suit on the wall, he turns to Chad and says, "That was quite the expedition wasn't it?"

Chad just shakes his head and says, "If I never have another adventure like that it'll be too soon for me."

James moves over and bends down to look at the damage to his robot, at least he hopes that's how it appears, but he is looking past his robot at Chads' robot, trying to spot the secret compartment that he saw earlier. He says, "That's a pretty nasty rip there. Are you going to be able to fix that, Brad?" He turns to look at Brad, waiting for an answer.

Brad strolls over and looking at the damaged area of the robot he says," Yeah I can fix it, but it's going to take a little while."

"Well, I'm off to clean up," says James before he turns and heads towards the hallway. He slaps Brad on the back as he turns to walk away.

"I'm going to help Brad clean off these robots before I get cleaned up," Chad replies.

James' step doesn't falter as he raises his eyebrows and then acknowledges the comment with a wave of his hand and continues down the hall. When he reaches the central area, he risks a glance over his shoulder and sees nothing but empty hallway behind him. He approaches Ashley and says, "Chad has a secret compartment on his robot."

Her mouth falls open, and she stands there gaping at James. She knows she must look foolish but is powerless to stop herself. "I saw him putting stuff in it at the gun store," says James, "and just now, I saw him pull out a dozen sticks of dynamite, some caps, some primer and a stunner like the one I asked you to hide."

"Well, it seems he hasn't given up on his idea to go to war with the zombies," she sighs.

"I just hope we don't regret his decision," says James. "He could end up killing us all in his bloodthirsty battle." Ashley nods and sits down at the table looking a little lost. James pulls up a chair and plops down into it across from Ashley. He reaches across the table and takes her hand.

Her eyes raise to meet his; they are filled with dreams for the future and a sense of something he can only describe as a fierce determination. Ashley is quite a girl, he thinks to himself, and a smile teases his lips. Ashley notices the smile and her mouth curves in a smile in response. "Thank you, I needed that," says Ashley.

James leans across the table and places a soft kiss on Ashley's lips and then says, "I need to go get cleaned up, I'll be back shortly." He raises and slowly releases her hand as he turns to head to the shower.

CHAPTER 5

Ashley remains sitting at the table contentedly thinking of the future. She's sure that if they could get away from all these zombies, she and James could have a real relationship. For now, she'll settle for the kisses and handholding he has been willing to do.

Brad finishes storing the dynamite, caps, and primer away and picks up the stunner. "This is the first electro-pulse-disabler I've seen," he says looking at Brad.

"Electro-what-what?" asks Chad.

Brad chuckles and says, "An electro-pulse-disabler—they call it that because it's powered by a self-charging cell. It shoots the electrical pulse in intervals. It's much like a semi-automatic rifle—and depending on the setting, it'll either stop you, drop you, or kill you." He turns it over in his hands, appreciating the metalwork of the casing.

Brad turns to store the electro-pulse-disabler in a little cubby he found under the bench. It's really just a wooden brace that runs across the back, but it forms a small shelf, well away from prying eyes. As he reaches in, his finger accidentally presses on the trigger. There is a whirring sound and then a sound like hissing air escaping—like when you unplug an air hose.

The electrical beam shoots out and, hitting the metal leg of the bench, redirects and hits Chad just above the ankle. Chad's mouth drops open, and he stands there starting to vibrate for about 30 seconds and then collapses to the floor in a heap. "Oh shit," exclaims Brad. He quickly stores the electro-pulse-disabler and runs over to Chad.

"I'm so, so sorry," he pleads with his fallen hero. After a minute or so, Chad stirs, and Brad breathes a sigh of relief. He wasn't sure if he had killed him or not until he moved.

"How the hell did that happen?" he asks looking at Brad.

"I was putting it away and accidentally pulled the trigger, and it bounced off the bench," Brad tells him. "I'm so, so sorry."

Chad shakes his arms and rotates his head then picks himself up off the floor. He twists and turns to make sure that everything is working correctly, then he turns and punches Brad in the shoulder. "If I didn't like you, that wouldn't have been in the shoulder," Chad says as Brad howls in pain. "Now, come on, and let's go see if they're ready to eat." He then turns and strides off. Brad rotates his shoulders and follows Chad down the hallway.

Brad notices Chad is limping slightly and asks, "Is your leg OK? You're limping a little bit."

Chad slows down and turns his head and says, "It's a little sore, but it'll be fine. No thanks to you."

"I'm sorry," Brad whines.

"Forget it," replies Chad. He slows his stride a little bit to minimize the limp so that he doesn't have to explain what happened.

As they enter the main area, Chad spies Ashley sitting at the table and wearing a cocky grin, he says, "Is it time to eat?"

Ashley's jaw drops momentarily, and then an icy look comes across her face as her eyes ignite with indignation. "It is not my job to feed you, just because I'm a woman," she screams at him.

"Chill, little darling," says Chad smirking smugly, "I didn't mean nothing by it."

"I'll show you chill," Ashley seethes at him.

"I think that will just about do the fireworks," James says as he enters the main area and comes to stand behind Ashley resting his hand on her shoulder. "Chad, I do believe you just volunteered you and Brad to cook this time."

The smug look flees from Chad's face, and his jaw slightly drops before he catches himself and says, "Yeah sure, we can do that."

As they move towards the kitchen area, James calls after them, "Don't forget that means washing the dishes afterward, too."

Ashley lowers her chin to her chest, closes her eyes, and mutters a simple, "I'm sorry."

James slips his arms around her waist, letting her lean back into him. Soon the warmth emanating from James and radiating through her body has all but erased the events of the previous few minutes from her mind. Her body relaxes and then James drops a kiss on her neck. Turning in the circle of his arms Ashley places a soft, gentle lingering kiss on his lips before easing back. "Thank you, again."

"Anytime," replies James, "I'm glad to see you were standing up for yourself and not letting that douche walk all over you."

"It's funny," remarks Ashley, "I was just waiting for you to get back and I was going to go cook up some patties."

"It won't hurt him to cook them, they're patties even he shouldn't be able to screw them up," comments James. Ashley giggles and returns to her seat at the table.

"Chad got hit with the electro-pulse-disabler," Ashley says.

James looks at her, the smile slipping from his face. "How do you know that?" he asks.

"I heard the whirring and the hiss, and when he came in here, he was limping but trying to hide it."

"I wonder if he did it himself or if Brad did it," James muses.

Ashley looks across the table at James and says, "I wanted to thank you for the help with my robot. I couldn't have done it without you."

"You're quite welcome for the help, but I think you could have done it quite fine on your own. I was just the grunt; you're the kickass engineer," James replies with a smile on his lips that shines out of his eyes.

"Well, let's just say it was a lot more enjoyable doing it with your help," she says as she smiles shyly at James.

"All I need now is the wireless transmitter, and then we'll be able to test it out," she says. "We can add it to our next mission," James responds.

Ashley reaches across the table and taking his hand in hers, raises her eyes to his and says, "I'm so glad I met you. If there's any reason I don't regret the zombie episode, even watching my parent's skin explode and having them try to eat me, it's because it all brought me to you."

"We don't have many patties left," Brad comments to Chad as he flips the patties again.

"I know," Chad replies, we have enough for a little bit yet, but we should plan another mission to find more food before they're all gone."

"Eventually we're going to run out of food sources," Brad says.

Chad looks at him and feels sorry for the worrisome youth, so he responds, "If we could get rid of the zombies it would not be such a challenge, and then we might be able to figure something out."

When the patties finish cooking, they gather up plates and cutlery and the patties and head out to the main area. They place the patties on the table and distribute the plates and cutlery. Chad turns to Ashley and says, "I'm sorry my comment earlier offended you. I didn't mean it to."

Ashley has all kinds of smart-ass comments run through her mind, and then she thinks for the sake of the unity of the team she should swallow them all. She simply replies, "Apology accepted."

They sit down to eat and discuss their options of whether they should stay and burn the city to rid it of the zombies, or if they should take a boat and try to go somewhere else where there might be more people. As usual, there have dividing opinions. Chad and Brad want to stay and kill all the zombies, while Ashley and James would like to see all the zombies dead, but they'd prefer to go somewhere where there are more people and fewer zombies.

"If we burn the city, our home such as it is, would be okay. It's far enough away from the other buildings," Chad states trying to convince Ashley and James to join his viewpoint. "Do you think the zombies are just going to stand there and watch you burn the city," James questions.

"No, probably not," agrees Chad, "but we have the guns and ammo now, and can hold them off while we set it."

"If they come at us in a group, like a mob that was at the gun store the other day, all the guns we have still wouldn't be enough to hold them off," James says.

They all have visions from that day jump into their mind, and it's a very sobering reminder of the level of danger they're facing. Ashley shivers remembering how she had forgotten it was the robot out there and not James himself.

After finishing their patties in silence, Chad and Brad pick up the dishes and head to the kitchen area wordlessly. James is staring off to space lost in thought, trying to devise a way to attach the guns to the robots in a way that they can use without the robots losing the use of their hands. Ashley studies James while he sits there staring off into space.

He's kind to me, she thinks, but he isn't overly into me. Maybe I should try pulling back a little. It might get his attention. I can't just come out and tell him how I feel. I've shown him, and now it's up to him, she decides. James notices Ashley looking at him and smiles at her as he says, "I think we should see what we can do to get those robots outfitted with some firepower."

Heading down to the work area they empty the bags of guns and ammo and are looking at all the different weapons they have. Ashley goes over to look at the arms of the robots trying to devise a way to mount them usefully. Chad and Brad stroll in from the hallway, and Chad says, "I think we should mount two guns on each robot."

"I don't think it would hurt to have the extra firepower," James agrees. Brad sidles over to Ashley, and they put their heads together trying to sort out how to mount the guns.

"We should use these shotguns," Chad says holding up a 12-gauge, "but I think we should saw the barrel off."

"That's actually a good idea," James agrees, "you lose some distance, but you gain a much wider spread."

He and Chad each grab two shotguns and head over to the bench and proceed to cut 20" off each barrel. "We have to attach them to the top to not interfere with the use of the hands," Brad says.

"How are we going to have them be able to pull the trigger, we'll have to use some sort of rod or pulley system," Ashley says.

"We also need to be able to reload them without taking them off," Chad points out.

"What if we mounted them like this?" James asks, holding one of the sawed-off shotguns above the robot's forearm low enough that when it is broken for reloading, the barrel has room to lower past the robot's hand.

"That could work," says Ashley, "and hooking up the trigger would be easier there, too."

James and Chad fill the helper rolls while Brad and Ashley do the designing. Working together they manage to get the guns attached to the robots. It's time to test them out, so Chad and James get suited up as Ashley says, "We can test them without ammo, you don't need to waste the ammo, and we don't need the noise attracting zombies."

Chad and James grunt their agreement as they struggle into the suits. Once they're all suited up Ashley switches on the robots, then Chad and James move them into position facing away from everyone just to be safe. They raise their arms and using the rods that were attached they fire the guns. They all go click. Then they break open the barrels and nod at each other.

"Awesome job, you two," James says. With the guns ready to go, they return the robots to their spot and shut them down.

Chad and James get unsuited and turn their attention to attaching the self-reloading hoppers that Ashley had designed. "That will make it much easier to reload them, all you have to do is keep the hoppers loaded," she says.

With the robots finished and realizing they haven't left the warehouse since they got there, James decides to go out and get some fresh air. Ashley decides to go with him, thinking just because I said it was up to him doesn't mean I can't give him lots of opportunities. Brad and Chad hang back; Chad wants to talk privately with Brad.

James looks out the window scanning the area outside, just to be safe, then unbolts the door and heads outside. Ashley steps out behind him, and they start walking. James heads towards the port wanting to see which boats seem best equipped. "I think that one would be the best," Ashley says pointing at a gleaming white boat tied to the dock.

Chad and Brad exit the warehouse and head in their direction.

As they approach, Chad wears a sardonic expression and says, "Still intent on leaving, aren't you?"

"With those generators, we found we can bring the robots with us," James replies. "That will increase our chances. Not sure how long they'll last, but it's a good start."

Deciding to let the matter drop for now Chad turns back towards the warehouse with Brad a step behind. James looks around, and after a quick look through the boat, he and Ashley return to the warehouse securing the door behind them.

CHAPTER 6

The day of the mission, they gather around the table in the central area of the warehouse to discuss the needs of the mission. Ashley brings the map to the table—they look at the map trying to decide where they need to go for each of the things they need. "Looks like we'll need to do a two-prong mission this time," James says.

"Yeah, these places are too far apart," Chad agrees, tapping the two sections of the city they had chosen.

"We'll stay together as long as possible," says James, "We're less vulnerable together."

"Agreed," nods Chad.

"Well, shall we get this show on the road?" says James as he stands and heads to the workroom to suit up and engage the robot. The others follow him down the hall.

James and Chad begin to suit up, and James asks, "Should we go to the area for the radio equipment and then you can continue on to get the food, or should we split off sooner and each go our own direction?"

"I think it would probably be best if we split up somewhere around that church," replies Chad while struggling into his suit.

"That probably would be a good spot to separate," agrees Ashley.

As James finishes suiting up, he says, "I'll meet you in the main area." He turns and follows his robot down the hall, making sure that the hopper is full of ammunition while he's at it. Ashley follows him down the hall and powers up the live feed so that she can help direct the guys. Chad follows down the corridor a few minutes later.

Brad heads directly to his station and, twisting some knobs watching the lights on the board, makes some adjustments. "Your robots are at max signal right now," he tells them.

Giving him a thumbs up, James says, "Off we go."

Ashley heads to the door and unlocks it, and as the robots do head out, she says, "Good luck, guys," and closes the door, making sure to secure the bolt.

She moves back to the live feed. She then begins scanning the route that the guys are going to take checking for zombies. James and Chad guide their robots through the gates, securing each one behind them, and then move into the fast run that their robots are capable of. Their journey to the edge of the built-up area is uneventful.

As they approach the built-up area's edge, Ashley says, "There're two small groups of zombies heading in your direction. It looks like the one coming straight at you has about 10, and the one coming from your left has only 4."

James shifts a bit to the left of Chad, and they continue on their way. It's only minutes, and they spot the zombies who speed into a run when they spot the robots.

"Let's hope that these guns work," says James.

"Let's kill them," snarls Chad. As the distance between them closes they enter the intersection of the cross street and James turns his head and sees the four zombies coming from that direction. He stops and raising his right arm fires that gun at the zombies coming straight at them. The pellets spread out and turn the four zombies on the edge of the group into a mass of bloody flesh that splatters on all the other zombies who keep coming. Chad raises both guns at once and fires them both as James fires his left gun at the zombies coming from the left. Chad's shot takes out half of the remaining zombies. The four coming from the left fall in a bloody tangle and lay there twitching. James fires his right gun at the remaining zombies, and as they fall, Chad yells, "Take that you flesh-eating freaks."

"Woohoo, these things work excellent. Good job you two," exclaims James. As they continue on their way, Chad has a huge smile on his face under the VR helmet. They make it to the church where they're going to part ways without further incident. "Be careful; this isn't the time to start a war," James cautions Chad before he veers off to head to the radio store and look for the wireless transmitter for Ashley's robot.

Chad waves as they part, but thinks to himself, "That's what you think; I'm going to kill every stinking zombie I see." Feeling powerful, he struts off on his way to get food. He does not bother performing the roof-to-roof approach.

As he gets closer, Ashley then says: "You should be adopting the roof approach—there's a small group of zombies one block west of you."

Chad pauses for a minute playing through the option of detouring to kill those zombies, but when the scene from the gun store flashes through his mind, he decides to save the zombie killing until after he completes his mission. Jumping up to the roof he continues his journey jumping from roof to roof until he reaches the store he hopes will hold the food they need.

James makes his approach to the radio store over the rooftops and easily slips inside. Cautiously he creeps down the ladder pausing to survey the store looking for lurking zombies. Finding the way clear he starts searching for the wireless transmitter. He sees a radio transmitter and thinking they could use it to contact other survivors somewhere he tucks it into his bag.

Making his way through the store, James comes across the wireless transmitter that Ashley requires to finish her robot. He tucks that into his bag and scans the shelves for a few minutes in case there is something else they could use. When he's satisfied that he has everything they need, he heads out of the store and starts making his way to the meeting spot.

Chad fills his bag with food smiling when he discovers some steaks in the freezer. He browses around and adds in a few bags of cookies for snacking on. Satisfied with his loot, he decides it's time to kill some zombies. He heads to the front door. "No need for subtlety this time," he thinks to himself.

As he exits the building, he sees a group of zombies a block south of him. He heads in their direction, and when he gets close enough, he brings up both guns and starts shooting shot after shot, pausing only when the self-reloading hopper needs refilling. The zombies are scrambling over their fallen companions that Chad shot, slipping and sliding in the blood and gore that's building up on the road.

Chad spins to the right blasting at the zombies as he turns. There is an explosion from the pump at the gas station. Chad pauses as an idea blooms in his head—he could make use of all the gas stations in the region to set the whole city on fire and kill all the zombies.

Chad returns to the present and sees zombies pouring in from all over. As memories from the day at the gun store flash through his mind Chad decides it would be better to save the fight for another day. He turns and starts running trying to evade the zombies.

While James is still a couple of blocks from the meeting place, Ashley says, "Chad is fighting a whole bunch of zombies."

"Direct me to him," James says without hesitation.

"Turn left," Ashley instructs. James takes a left and makes use of the super-fast speed of his robot.

Chad keeps firing both guns dropping zombies like flies, and it's all he can do to keep his hopper full. He begins retreating while continuing to shoot both weapons at the zombies. He looks around trying to find a place where he can escape. He knows he needs to get out of there soon or he's going to be overwhelmed.

James is speeding towards Chad and Ashley is guiding him with the live feed. As he rounds the last corner, he sees Chad and can't believe the multitude of zombies that are chasing him.

CHAPTER 7

"We should go get that food put away," says Ashley.

"Maybe we should cook some of it up, too; I'm kind of hungry," Brad says sheepishly.

Ashley smiles and says, "I'll cook something up as soon as I get everything put away."

"I'll give you a hand," says James. They head off side by side down the tunnel in companionable silence.

As they walk with arms softly swinging at their sides, their hands touch each other—and James, for the first time in his life, feels like he just brushed his hand against a live electrical wire. Ashley blushes—she can feel the heat rising into her cheeks, but it is nothing compared to the excitement she felt when their hands brushed.

As they reach the table in the central area, James says, "I found a communication radio—maybe after we eat, we should set it up and see if it works."

"That's a great idea—and great thinking, James! We might be able to communicate with other survivors." They ignore the bag with the radios for now, and James picks up the bag of food that Chad had brought back and heads for the kitchen.

"I never got to ask Chad what kind of food he managed to find," says James.

"I was too busy watching the live feed and trying to keep track of you," says Ashley with a smile on her face.

As James glances over at her, he notices how beautiful she is—how soft her skin looks. He can't help thinking she looks good with the blush on her cheeks, too, before he shakes his head as they continue towards the kitchen.

As they sort through the supplies that Chad managed to find, James lets out a low whistle, and Ashley chuckles when she comes across the bags of cookies. Deciding that she will make a meal fit for a king, Ashley keeps out some potatoes, vegetables, and four of the monster steaks. "We'll eat well tonight," she says to James.

James has a sudden vision of living with Ashley—and this being part of their daily routine—and not sure what to make of it or where it's coming from, he shakes his head and looks over the selection of food Chad managed to obtain.

"This is awesome," James says as he begins taking out the pots and pans that they'll need for preparing the dinner. He begins peeling the potatoes, while Ashley starts the vegetables and preps the steaks. While Ashley monitors the steaks, James leans against the counter watching her with a distant look in his eyes. It's not long before Brad and Chad, smelling the steaks frying, come wandering into the kitchen.

"Those smell absolutely awesome," Chad exclaims.

"Good job on the eats," James says to Chad.

"We'll set the table," Brad offers.

Chad turns to stare at him, and then as scenes from his encounter with the zombies do flash across his mind, he smiles and says, "Sure, why not?"

As Chad and Brad grab plates and cutlery and head for the table, James mashes the potatoes and transfers them to a serving bowl. Ashley places the steaks on a plate and strains the vegetables before depositing them into a container. James picks up the bowl of vegetables, and they exit the kitchen and head to the table.

As they approach the table, they see that one of the guys had found a piece of material that was now serving duty as a tablecloth. It didn't quite fit, but it was big enough to cover the area they used for eating. "Nice touch with the table cloth," Ashley smirks as she walks over and places the steaks in the center of the table.

"Thanks, I thought that with such a good meal, we should at least make the table look a little more normal," Brad replies sheepishly.

"Thank you for finding some excellent food, Chad. It sure beats McDonald's patties and fries," Ashley says.

Performing a mock bow, Chad lit up his face with a smile as he replies, "At your service, madam."

Everybody laughs, and Ashley thinks it's too bad he's such a douche—he can be quite good looking when he's smiling.

James, not sure where the notion comes from, pulls out Ashley's chair for her and as she sits he slides it in for her. He's not sure why, but it is important to him that he not be upstaged by Chad in front of Ashley. Smiling he takes his seat and says, "Pass the steak please." Everyone chuckles and then digs into the delicious meal laid out before them.

During the meal, they keep the mood light and steer away from any conversation that will raise tension. The group all relish the familial feeling that tugs at each of them. Chad thinks to himself, "I wish it could be like this all the time," and then upon deciding just to enjoy it while it lasts, he pushes all negative thoughts from his mind. Brad is pretty quiet eating his meal with a slight smile on his lips.

After the meal finished and the dishes cleaned and put away, James follows Ashley out of the kitchen area and has to struggle to keep his eyes off her wiggling bottom just in front of him. As his fists clench at his side, he realizes he hasn't been successful, and he wonders what has come over him.

As they approach the table, James moves so he is walking side by side with Ashley. He can't understand this sudden desire to keep turning his head and glancing at her. The feeling of happiness when she smiles at him - it's like he's addicted to her or something. He ponders these feelings as he walks silently beside her.

James grabs the bag with the radio and Ashley's wireless transmitter for her robot and heads to the work area. Ashley stays in step with him as they stroll down the hallway, and Brad and Chad are already in the work area. As he walks by Chad and Brad, James notices that they are looking at maps of the city, and can just imagine what they're planning.

"I think those two are planning something," James whispers to Ashley.

"You're probably right. They're probably planning to burn the city or something," Ashley whispers back. "Let's not worry about it right now though, ok?" James looks at her for a moment before nodding his head in agreement.

James withdraws the radio from the bag and sets it aside while

Ashley takes the wireless transmitter and heads over to her robot. James heads over to give Ashley a hand with her robot if she needs it. She has him help hold things while she attaches the wireless transmitter and gets it hooked up to her robot. "I think that should about do it," Ashley says withdrawing her hands from inside her robot.

"What's this for?" James asks motioning to a small box he hadn't seen on the robots he and Chad were using.

"That's for the XR box," Ashley says. "It gives my robot extended reality. And this," she says pointing to a bigger box-shaped thing on the other side of the robot, "is the quantum computing."

Staring in awe, James says, "So this will be like some sort of super robot?"

"Yes, that's the plan," replies Ashley.

"I've also added in some artificial intelligence to it," Ashley says with a hint of pride in her voice.

"What does that do for it," James enquires.

"It's kind of like the traction control and lane assist in some of the older vehicles," Ashley explains. "If I had time, I could make it fully automated and voice controlled."

James' mouth drops in awe, "Wow, beautiful and smart," he says before he thinks, and then he blushes.

"Thank you," breathes Ashley.

Chad and Brad have located all the gas stations on the map of the city, and Chad whispers, "We should start here, pointing to a spot on the map, "and blow up this one, then work our way back like this," drawing more lines on the map with his finger. "We should light each one with a long enough fuse that we'll be well away from it before it blows up. Then the zombies will be drawn to the noise of it while we're heading to the next station," Chad points out.

"How are you going to do this by yourself?" Brad asks.

"I'm not," replies Chad. "You're going to use the other robot and help me. I'll do one side of the city, and you'll do the other side."

"I don't know if I can do that," says Brad.

"Sure, you can," says Chad. "Remember: you won't actually be out there with the zombies even though it will seem like it. The worst that can happen is they'll get the robot."

Chad is so excited at the thought of killing all the zombies that he can hardly contain it. He is almost dancing as he stares at the map, seeing instead how he thinks the attack on the zombies will play out. He can picture the gas stations exploding flinging hundreds of zombies screeching into the air to land on the grass and burn. Some of them further away blow up in a mass of blood and bone. It doesn't hurt that he envisions him and Brad returning from their mission and him being the hero for killing all the zombies.

Ashley during a break from working on the robot strolls over to the bench and picks up the radio James had brought back with her wireless transmitter. "This was an excellent idea to bring the radio back," she says to James.

"Thank you! I was trying to look for anything that could be of use to us, and I thought maybe we could communicate with other survivors with it," James explains.

As she switches it on the sound of static fills the room, and she bounces up and down in her excitement before turning to look at James, noticing a different expression in his eyes. James wraps his arms around Ashley and pulls her close. The smell of her hair and the closeness has a strange effect on him, and he suddenly realizes as he feels the tightening in his chest that he really likes this girl. He lowers his mouth to hers his lips seeking and containing all the promise he feels in his chest. Unbeknownst to him, the feeling in his chest is the beginning roots of love, and the hope he has always had for a beautiful, peaceful place to live blossoms in its company.

Ashley feels the difference in the kiss and eagerly responds, answering promise for a promise. Her hope swells so much she can hardly contain it. Just as Ashley is about to lose herself in the kiss, the kiss she has been longing for so long for James to initiate, the radio which had been left on scan blasts out, "Help! If anyone out there hears this message, this is Karen. We have a community of survivors stationed in Hakodate. We are managing the zombies due to the lower number of them. To survive though, we need help killing off the rest of them and farming and gathering resources. I hope someone hears this or our whole colony could be doomed."

They all stand in shocked silence staring at the radio. James and Ashley feel their hope grow even stronger. Chad and Brad have a feeling of inevitable doom. Chad determines to make sure he gets his chance to kill the zombies before being forced to desert the city.

Ashley tries to respond over and over but receives no answer. They all stand around lost in their own thoughts as the tension in the room rises. Chad wants to stay and kill all the zombies, and he knows James and Ashley are going to want to go. The tension in the room rises until it is so thick to the point that you could cut it with a knife.

"I think we should go and help them," says James. "This is a perfect opportunity to have fewer zombies to deal with and more people to do it with."

Chad huffs out a reply, "I knew you were going to say that. Let's stay here and deal with our own zombies and let them fend for themselves. They've made it this far, and besides as far as we know they might be gone already. They did say their whole colony could collapse."

"Just how do you come up with the idea that it's better to stay here and face more zombies with fewer people?" James asks Chad.

"Look at what we have here, we have a full robot control center, and all the video games you could ever want. Not to mention the cool chill spots we have made out of those shipping containers and our hammocks. We don't even know what they have there, we could end up a lot worse off than we are," responds Chad sullenly.

"I hate change," Chad thinks to himself. "It's bad enough that we had to change when these stupid zombies came—the only change I want is when they're all dead.

"I think we should go help," says Ashley. "How would you feel if we had issued the request for help and nobody came?"

"I think we should kill all the zombies," chimes in Brad. "Maybe then, things can go back to normal," he thinks to himself. Even with the warehouse and having met Chad, James, and Ashley, he wishes things were normal. "Chad seems to be so strong—he must be, right?" he thinks. Why should we abandon our city to them and not even know where we're going to end up?" Brad finishes off.

"It could end up being better than what we have here," James retorts.

CHAPTER 8

"If we got there and it was worse than here, we wouldn't necessarily have to stay long," Ashley points out.

"It's not like they're the only place in the world besides Tokyo," James adds in.

"But look what we've done here since we've been here," Chad whines.

James thinks to himself, "I don't understand this guy. We did it here, and we can do it again."

"I'm going to try again," says Ashley. "They probably don't have time to sit and monitor for a call that might not come." As she heads over to the radio to call again, they all fall silent—each with their own thoughts.

Brad is thinking about what things were like before the zombies came, and he wishes it could go back to that. He's torn between sticking with Chad and siding with James and Ashley, but he really doesn't like change. At least with Chad, if they killed all the zombies, they'd still be in a familiar place.

Chad thinks that he hates the zombies, and he wants to stay here and kill them all and take back everything that they took from him. "Besides," he reasons with himself, "if there's no one else around because they all turned into zombies, I could take back more than what they stole from me, and no one would complain."

James thinks that he could finally get the beautiful place he wanted to live, and with fewer zombies, they could be killed off more easily with more people. He believes that as appealing as this dream still is to him, it pales in comparison to the thought of having a real relationship with Ashley. Still relatively new to him, these feelings have almost taken control of him.

As Ashley is trying to connect with the people that sent the message, her thoughts are running parallel to James'. She remembers his dream of a beautiful place to live with more people and fewer zombies. She hopes that their being together might make it even more attractive to him.

She repeatedly tries for about ten minutes to reach the people that had issued the call for help. Realizing that it is probably futile, she decides to take a break, at least. "I still think that we should go and help them," she says to the group.

"Even if we got there and they have been overtaken," says James, "we will know that we tried to help. If there are fewer zombies there than here, we could kill them all more easily."

Chad shakes his head, "Are you even listening to yourself?" he asks. "If they couldn't kill them all, what makes you think we could?"

"First of all, we don't know that they haven't held their own or even wiped out the zombies," James says, "and they may not have the guns and ammo that we do."

"Yeah, but if we go," complains Chad, "we have to leave behind everything that we've done here."

"Where do you stand in all this, Brad?" James asks. "You haven't said much."

Brad swallows as all eyes turn to look at him—he wishes he could fall through the floor and disappear. He hates being the center of attention, but his loyalty to Chad combined with his dislike of change combine to enable him to blurt out, "I think we should stay here and kill all the zombies. We know what we have here, and everything the zombies took from us is here. They should deal with their own damn zombies."

Everyone remains quiet, still looking at Brad. Chad feels terrible for Brad and decides to take the scrutiny off of him. "I don't think it would be too smart to leave everything we have here to go help someone who for all we know could already be dead," he says. As Ashley and James turn to look at him, and he can see Brad visibly relax.

"In case you haven't noticed," James says, "most of the stuff here that we've accumulated or made use of isn't bolted to the floor, and we can take a lot of the necessary stuff with us."

"Besides that," pipes up Ashley, "this is all just stuff, it's certainly not more important than somebody's life."

"Maybe to you—I don't even know these people," Chad hurls back.

Everybody falls silent at Chad's outburst, stunned into silence at the lack of feeling he has for other human beings. Chad doesn't even have the decency to look sorry for what he said. With raised eyebrows, James stares at Chad for a long moment before replying, "I think that is honestly the most horrendous thing I have ever heard anyone say."

Ashley opens and closes her mouth repeatedly, but can't get any words to come out. Finally, she just shakes her head and turns away.

Silence descends on the warehouse for a few moments, during which Chad watches as James walks over to Ashley and places his hand on her shoulder. He realizes then that it's not just teaming up against him, but that Ashley chose James over his advances when he first arrived. In his mind she should be with him, he was here first.

"If you two love birds think you can save the world, because you're looking at everything through rose-colored glasses, feel free to go," yells Chad.

"What is or isn't between Ashley and me isn't any of your concern," James yells back at Chad.

"Your jealousy won't help anything," says Ashley. "You didn't actually think I wouldn't see through those cheesy pickup lines you tried when you first got here did you?"

"All this fighting isn't getting us anywhere," Brad interjects.

James turns and looks at Brad and realizes that he is not a strong personality—he can't fault him for falling under Chad's show of strength. "Even if it's phony," James says, as he realizes Chad is all bluster and nothing else. Chad likes to puff up and beat his chest and make lots of noise, thinks James, "What a sad individual." He almost feels pity for him—almost.

"No Brad, it isn't," James agrees, "but Chad can't seem to understand that human life should take priority—and even if you burn the city, where are the zombies going to go? They're not just going to stand there and burn. You'll push them right to us."

"The explosions would kill most of them," Chad says before realizing he is exposing his plan. "The rest would burn in the ensuing fire," he finishes.

"I think your hatred of the zombies and your thirst for revenge is coloring your vision," James retorts.

Switching subjects Ashley asks, "Since when is loving somebody such a bad thing? You accuse us of wanting to save the world, is that really such a bad thing wanting to help other people so everybody can have a better life?"

It's Chad's turn to stand there opening and closing his mouth, looking like a fish out of the water.

"The one thing I do know as far as this subject goes," continues Ashley, "is that we are stronger together as a group. To divide that strength wouldn't be in the best interest of anybody."

They all think about that for a minute as silence once again descends on the warehouse penetrated only by the static of the radio. James doesn't want to admit he needs Chad and Brad, Brad not so much, but he is also honest enough with himself to accept that she is right.

"She is wrong; I could do this on my own," is what is running through Chad's mind. Even though he knows deep down that he hates being on his own, he craves companionship even if it's not the people he would usually have chosen. He keeps his thoughts from traveling that deep while holding on to his hate and desire for revenge.

Brad is thinking about the previous missions they have done, and how James and Chad have automatically had each other's backs even though they disagree. He can see how each of them would have lost their robot without the other one stepping in to help. She has a point he thinks, but he is so unwilling to change that he can't allow the logic of her statement to sway his loyalty to Chad.

"I acknowledge that we do have more strength together," says Chad. "That doesn't mean that Brad and I have to cave to your desire to go off saving the world looking for some romantic retreat."

"I'm not looking for some romantic retreat," says Ashley, "I'm looking for someplace with fewer zombies so that they can be eliminated and we can build a life."

"You need to stay focused on the issue at hand and never mind my romantic life, Chad—it in no way involves you, so it isn't your concern," says Ashley adamantly.

"Would it be so bad for you to at least consider our position?" James asks Chad, "if you set aside your hatred of the zombies and your thirst for revenge? It might make sense to you."

"What doesn't make sense to me is why we want to run away and let the zombies win," Chad replies.

"Staying and letting them kill us changes that how?" James asks.

"I don't plan to stay and let them kill me," huffs Chad.

James looks at Chad unblinkingly, before saying, "That's the dumbest thing I've ever heard. Nobody ever plans to stay and be killed. It doesn't mean it won't happen; you need to get a reality check man."

"At least then, I would die while trying to protect what's ours," Chad says. "Think about it, man—there's nobody else here. If we eliminate the zombies, we can have anything we want in the whole city."

"So you not only want what was yours before the zombies,"

James says quietly, "but you also want to profit off everybody else's loss?"

"That is cold," Brad thinks to himself, "but he has a point. If there's nobody else around, we could be in charge when other people come seeking refuge. We could be like Kings." The thought brings a smile to his face and strengthens his resolve to stick with Chad.

"What, should I just leave it for other people coming to seek refuge to take," asks Chad, "How the hell does that make any sense?"

"It makes perfect sense," replies James, "It's called working in harmony."

"Well it's not my job to look after the rest of the world," Chad retorts.

"So what's your plan for killing all the zombies?" Ashley asks of Chad, "and if you burn the whole city, how much stuff do you think there'll be that's usable? All you're going to gain is a bunch of charred rubbish," she says as she walks over and huffs as she leans against the bench.

Chad thinks about that for a minute, admitting that he forgot that if he burned the city,the all would be rubble. "Still, we could rebuild it," he thinks, not considering where they would get the materials to do the rebuilding.

"Even if you burn the city and kill all the zombies, which I don't personally think will play out the way you envision, you're still not going to gain back what you lost when they came, because you're going to destroy it along with them," Ashley says trying to reason with an unreasonable douche.

Brad contemplates this latest twist on things and wonders what the point of killing the zombies is if they're still not only going to lose everything they always lost but all the resources they had been using to stay alive thus far. "Where would we get food," he wonders?

Chad, sensing Brad's wavering loyalty, refuses to admit the validity of Ashley's statement. "I don't want to go and lose the security we have here," states Chad, "or the hammocks. Those are cool—and all the video games. We could end up with nothing, James."

"Those are all things that can be replaced, Chad," James responds. "People's lives can't be replaced."

"I can't believe you're fighting to stay in a city that you're just going to destroy instead of helping people," Ashley butts in. "If we stay, you'll end up killing all of us."

"It's true," says James. "During all our missions we have taken steps to ensure we didn't lead the zombies here, and now you want to chase them all to us."

"And when they all come running here," Ashley pleads, "there's nowhere for us to run to."

"Do you think that could really happen," Brad whimpers, "that they could outrun the fire and head right to us?"

"Damn it, Brad! That's not going to happen. I told you how it was going to happen. Are you going to listen to these two lovebirds who can't stand anything other than love and flowers or me? I walked you through how it would go," Chad yells.

Brad is cowed by Chad's anger and stammers, "No, Chad. I was just wondering if they knew what they were talking about."

"You honestly think because we want to go help some people, and we're attracted to each other that we don't see all the death and danger we face every day?" James asks.

"You don't want to see it," Chad retorts. "That's why you want to run away."

"That makes us bad to want to live where there are less or no zombies," Ashley screams. "Then why are you so gung-ho to kill them all Chad?"

Having no answer, Chad simply says, "This is useless," before turning and stalking off. Brad quickly follows.

As their footsteps fade away silence once again descends on the warehouse, and the tension dissipates. "I can't believe him," Ashley says to James.

"It's alright, Ash," James says as he rubs his hand up her back, "let's just make our plans for getting out of here. Those people need help, and if he burns the city, we'll need to escape."

CHAPTER 9

James and Ashley are in the warehouse looking over a map to pick out their best route to Hakodate. "I think this would be our best route," James says as he draws a line on the map.

"That looks like the most direct one," Ashley agrees.

"Let's make a list of what we need to take, and we'll get up early and start loading the boat," James says.

"Ok, do you want to take the robots?" Ashley asks.

At James' affirmative, she writes them down. They cover many other necessities and some non-essentials to keep Chad and Brad happy if they come along.

"Some of the things he has brought up in our arguments are all the video games and the hammocks," James says.

Ashley adds them to the list. "Is there anything that Brad seems to be really connected to?" she asks.

"I can't say that there really is anything that seems to catch his attention," James comments. "He always seems just to follow Chad around."

"After we have the boat loaded, you should talk to Chad and Brad and try and compromise with them so that they'll come along. If we leave them here, James, they're going to die," Ashley pleads.

"I will speak to them as soon as we have the boat loaded," James promises.

"Thank you," Ashley says placing a soft kiss on Chad's lips.

"You guys fight like you're a bunch of girls, you know?"

"That's because half of the fighting is about this beautiful girl," James says as he runs his hand up Ashley's back and, hooking it behind her neck, pulls her in for a kiss.

"You already have this girl," she winks, "so there's no need to fight about that."

"I think we should call it a night so that we can get an early start," James says with a smile on his lips.

Ashley doesn't say a thing but takes his hand and, switching off the work light, turns and heads back to their room.

Chad spends a couple of hours with Brad talking in his room. "We don't need them," he says. "We can do this ourselves."

"What if they're right and we end up chasing the zombies here?" Brad asks.

"That's why we'll do it early in the morning," Chad says. "They'll be loading stuff on the boat, and we can sneak the robots out, and we'll have it done before they know we're doing it. If it goes wrong, we'll just get on the boat with them—but at least, we'll have tried."

Brad is relieved that Chad is finally acknowledging the possible scenario put forward by James. It seems that he may have been thinking more about it than he was letting on. He wonders if his backup plan is what he really said, or if he just said that to keep him happy. "Oh well," he decides, "at least, there is a backup plan."

After Brad agrees Chad promises to wake Brad up once James and Ashley are gone. He heads to his room and calls it a night. Brad has trouble getting to sleep. Nervous about getting found out and excited to get to help Chad kill all the zombies. Finally, he dozes off and sleeps fitfully for the rest of the night.

Ashley and James are awake almost as soon as the sun is up the next morning. Walking quietly so as not to wake Chad and Brad they head to the kitchen and grab a few cookies for a quick breakfast. Finished their makeshift breakfast they head to the work area to start loading the things on their list onto the boat.

Chad wakes up, and as he glances out his door, he spies Ashley and James exiting the kitchen area and heading to the work area. We'll need to bring the robots and the suits up to the main area, he thinks, there will be less chance of being noticed too soon that way. Quietly he moves over to Brad's door and turns the knob.

"I think we should load everything except the robots," says James. "We can leave them until we're ready to go. Just in case we need them."

"That's a good idea," Ashley agrees, "and it'll give you more credibility in trying to compromise with them." Having decided that they begin loading things. They work consistently and make good progress.

Brad and Chad making two trips timed to miss Ashley and James when they are in the warehouse, maneuver both robots with their control suits to the main area. They lay the control suits on the table, and Chad heads back to get the dynamite, caps, and primer. He is so excited his body is vibrating with the effort to control it.

"What should we do about loading the food," Ashley says, "should we get it loaded, or wait until we're ready to leave to load it?"

"I think we should probably wait until after I talk to Chad and Brad about coming," James says. "Otherwise, it'll turn into another argument."

James turns to Ashley and asks, "What do you think we should do about the tools?"

"Should we take them, and if so, which ones?" Ashley walks over to the bench in the work area and looks over the tools. She looks around the work area contemplating which would be the most necessary ones to have. "I do not think that we can take them all," she says. "There is only limited space on the boat."

She begins sorting them into two sections on the bench, one to take with them, and one to leave behind. James watches her sorting for a minute and begins to help sort the rest, thinking he understands how she's sorting them. Soon, they have reduced the number of essential tools to a small section capable of fitting in one of the crates they had found.

Chad and Brad suit up in the control suits—and sneaking the robots out the back of the warehouse so that it will be between them and the ship Ashley and James are loading stuff onto, they set off for the city. Chad is eager to put his plan into action, but not wanting a confrontation beforehand urges Brad to walk quietly—until they are out of sight of the warehouse. Then they start running and reach the city in no time.

They separate and each head for their assigned stations armed with explosives and get ready to end the zombies in one fell swoop. Brad is nervous as he heads off, but it helps to know

Chad is beside him in the other control suit, and it is just the robot out there risking encountering the zombies. He focuses on mounting the first explosive as Chad had shown him.

Moving to the cabin to see if he can get the boat running, James turns to Ashley and says, "It's too bad we can't try again to contact the people that sent that message."

"It would be nice," agrees Ashley, "but I already put the wireless transmitter in my robot, and it's hooked up and set up for the suit now. The radio would let us hear messages, but we have no way of communicating now."

"It's okay," says James as he touches the right wires together and the boat rumbles to life. Ecstatic that it worked, James turns to Ashley who moves into his arms, a big smile lighting up her face.

"Awesome, James," she breathes just before his lips descend on hers. As she deepens the kiss, James grasps the bottom of her shirt and lifts it up. Just as her shirt passes her belly button, there is a huge explosion.

Regretfully, James releases her shirt, and they pull apart looking at each other before heading outside to see what is happening. As they come out of the ship, they both suddenly stop as Ashley exclaims, "Holy shit!" She is staring at the huge plume of smoke circling over the city.

"You can see the flames from here," James says. "It must be one hell of a fire. We better go see what those two are up to in there," he adds.

They run over to the warehouse and having to enter through the work area because all the other doors are still locked, they rush to the main area and skidding to a halt, James blurts out,

"What the fuck are you guys doing? Why on earth are you even in my robot suit, Brad? You suck at controlling the robots—that's why you don't have one. You better fucking get it back here before you get it killed by the zombies."

Ashley places her hand on James' back trying to calm him down as Chad begins to explain their plan. "We started on the far side of the city," he explains, "and we are working our way back this way. That way, when we set the last one, we can run back here."

"Our lives are at stake just as much as yours," Ashley screams at Chad.

"You could have at least told us you were doing this," James adds in.

"You said you didn't want anything to do with it," Chad reminds them. "We figured that we'd just do it on our own."

"Just because we didn't agree with what you were doing doesn't give you the right to not at least alert us to what you were doing so we could be prepared when it blows up in our faces," James says.

James begins getting into the control outfit for Ashley's robot as Ashley moves over to the live feed to see what is going on. "Holy Shit!" she exclaims for the second time since exiting the ship. "The fire is huge," she says. "There are burning zombies jumping out of buildings, and there are thousands of them running away."

"Yeah!" exclaims Chad.

"Did you even think of the fact that you're going to burn all the food we could have made use of?" Ashley yells at Chad.

"Actually," Brad pipes up, "there was a shipping container with a refrigerator unit on it that contained tons of meat. We already stocked up on as much as we could."

"That's great," retorts Ashley, "but it's not going to last forever!"

As she turns back to the live feed, Ashley notices Chad and Brad are both on the move again, and asks, "Where the hell are you going now?"

"Off to the next station," Chad explains. "We each have three to blow up, and it will form a diamond shape around the city. It should make it possible to burn the entire city and kill all the zombies," Chad gloats.

As she turns back to the live feed, Ashley can't believe Chad would start these fires without talking to them. Sure, she thinks, she and James had loaded the ship, but they were planning to talk to Chad and Brad before they just sailed off. She remembers the last few moments on the ship before the blast. She sure wishes Chad had at least waited a while longer to start blowing up gas stations.

James is still pissed that Brad is using his robot, without permission I might add, he thinks to himself. He still can't help thinking what he and Ashley would be doing right now if Chad hadn't started blowing things up. "Focus," he reminds himself. "The main goal right now needs to be getting the robots home safely."

"You know," James begins, "as soon as the ship was loaded, I was going to come and talk to you and try to compromise with you. That's why we left the robots off the ship."

"Like I'm a mind reader," Chad retorts.

"We need to put this petty bickering aside for now," Ashley chimes in. "I swear, you two fight just like a couple of school girls."

Brad can't help the chuckle that escapes as he then pictures James and Chad dressed in dresses standing on the school steps screaming at each other. "I'm glad that you find it so amusing," Chad turns on him.

"I'm sorry, Chad," Brad says still chuckling, "but it does bring to mind a pretty funny picture."

"I guess it would at that," sighs James.

Remembering what Ashley had said on the ship about not needing to fight about her, James realizes his anger toward Chad has suddenly dropped to an all-time low. "As soon as I'm suited up here, I'll come and help you guys," James says to Chad.

"I'm good for now," Chad says, "but you can go over and help Brad."

Their plan calls for them to blow up the stations simultaneously and Chad figures if James helps Brad he won't have to wait so long for him before lighting his fuse. James finishes suiting up, and Ashley turns away from the live feed to switch on the robot. James is already familiar with the controls she has installed because he helped her work on it, and she explained it all to him in detail while they worked.

As she heads to the door to open it for him, she says to James, "Be careful out there."

"Of course," responds James. As he heads out the door, he runs out to the main road into the city and turning towards the city he gives the robot all it's got. Ashley is impressed as she watches the live feed, calling out directions to James.

"Take your next right," she calls out. James reaches the intersection and turns right.

"Why the hell is he turning already?" Chad mutters.

Hearing the mutter, Ashley is proud to reply, "It's because he'll be at the station in about two minutes."

"What the hell?" Chad yelps—astonished at how quickly James has gotten there.

James streaks to the gas station and, as he skids to a halt, sees Brad ambling his way and says, "Hurry up, Brad! Let's get this one set up."

CHAPTER 10

While James is waiting, crouched down behind a gas pump for concealment, for Brad to get to the second station, he notices that there are a lot more zombies than they have ever seen before. "The mass of zombies out here now makes that swarm at the gun store look like a walk in the park," he says.

"I didn't know that there would be this many," Chad says as he waits for James and Brad to get their station ready.

"Are you starting to see why I said this was a bad idea?" James asks. "It is quite likely starting a war that we can't win."

"We're not trying to fight them hand to hand or even with guns," Chad says. "That's what all the fire is for."

"Not yet—we're not," James agrees, "but that is going to come. I just hope we survive it."

Like James, Chad is crouched behind a pump for concealment, with the primer in his hand ready to stretch it out and light it as soon as they're ready. Finally, Brad arrives saying, "Where the hell did all these zombies come from?"

Chuckling James replies, "Out of the woodwork, I guess."

With Brad helping, they get the explosives set up in no time. "Let's get going," James says to Chad, and they begin stretching out the primer.

"On three," says Chad, and begins counting, "One, two, three." As he reaches three, he and Brad bend down and light the fuse.

Then, turning, they all begin running to the next station.

"This station is a lot bigger," Brad says as they run, "It's going to be a much bigger explosion than the other one."

"That's why we need to get far enough away," James replies. "The blast if we were too close could incapacitate our robots."

"Shit," Chad utters, "I never thought of that."

"Everybody up," Ashley calls out, and Chad and James instantly jump up and climb onto a building roof. Brad hesitates for an instant, not sure what is happening—and as understanding dawns, James follows up onto the roof. They continue their trip going from roof to roof and then pause to watch the huge explosion and the curling ball of fire that causes another surge of more zombies.

"Holy shit!" Chad exclaims. "There's even more of them." Some zombies are being thrown from the buildings by the force of the blast, while others are being thrown into the building or mashed against the wall. There are still swarms of zombies pouring out the doors and windows of the building—adding to the horde that is already racing around on the streets below.

They are preparing to head to the next station when all the sudden there is a banging on the door. Everybody instantly falls silent. They all instinctively know that they can't make any noise, or the zombies will go into horde mode. That would be the end for them all, and what a grisly end it would be.

"I told you it would come to this," James says to Chad.

"How the hell did they come here?" Chad whispers back.

"I don't know, but we need to figure out how to deal with this,"

Ashley suggests in a haggard whisper. Brad whimpers but doesn't say anything.

"We need to get back to the warehouse as quickly as possible," James urgently whispers to them and leaping off the roof he streaks toward the port house.

"I'm coming," Brad replies as he quickly follows suit and James slows enough to let him catch up.

Chad is determined to get his last gas station and despite the urging from the others heads for the station instead of retreating to the port house. "I can still get my last station," he says. "We've come this far, no point letting them win now."

"That'll just add even more zombies to the number we already have to deal with," James chastises Chad.

Ashley quietly moves from door to door installing the barricades they had made up for just such an instance like this. Finally finishing with the last one she grabs a pump shotgun and comes back to stand by the guys. If anyone had taken the time to look at her, they would know by her stance and the expression on her face, that she was ready to kill. "I'm as ready as I can be," she says.

Everyone is scared as fuck, and the tension is riding high as they continue to argue with Chad in whispers to come back home. "I can get this last station, I know it," Chad fiercely whispers. "Maybe the explosion will draw them away."

"Or maybe it will just send even more here; I told you that this would happen," James vehemently whispers.

"Chad, it's enough," James scolds. "You've had your chance now come and help deal with the mess."

"I know that I can get this one," Chad insists. "I'm almost there."

"That's just like adding fuel to the fire," James retorts. "Did you forget that you are in this warehouse, too? It won't be just us they kill if they get in."

As James and Brad approach the port house, they suddenly skid to a halt as James fiercely whispers, "There are a lot more zombies at the gates, ready to break them down."

"There's no choice," he says to Brad. "Open fire!"

James and Brad begin firing into the zombies. "How the hell do they know we're in here," Brad pleads.

"They don't," James replies to him. "If they knew we were in here, they'd be breaking in already."

The ones being blown to bits are covering the other ones in blood and gore, and some of the zombies are knocked down with the flying remains being briefly buried in the bloody mess. The zombies climbing out from under the mutilated remains look extremely daunting with the blood and gore dripping off them. It doesn't take long for the zombies to get agitated and they quickly begin to swarm the robots.

Still whispering James urges Brad to keep moving to avoid being swarmed, "Don't stop firing at them while you're moving," he reminds him. Avoiding the swarming zombies, the two keep pumping round after round into them but even as the leading zombies are obliterated the horde of zombies just keeps coming.

Suddenly Ashley exclaims in a terrified whisper, "They're banging on the barricades trying to break in."

"I'm sorry, Ash, but there's nothing we can do, all this ruckus has attracted even more zombies," James says to her. "You need to get your ass back here and help out Chad," James demands.

"Come on," pleads Ashley. "You're the one that caused this mess."

All of a sudden forgetting the need to whisper, Chad exclaims, "Son of a bitch! They got my robot."

"Well, that's certainly not going to help any," James hisses at him. Chad immediately begins getting out of the control outfit and runs over to grab a gun and gets set to help Ashley in the fight for their lives.

"Someone should pack up some food because we're going to have to run for it," James states.

"Why the hell haven't you loaded the food on your ship yet?" Chad seethes at James.

"Because you were so single-mindedly intent on causing this mess, that I had to try and convince you to come before I knew how much to load," James loudly whispers back at him.

"That doesn't really matter now," Ashley puts in. "Let's get it packed," she says to Chad.

Chad and Ashley scramble to pack as much food as they can carry as they try to figure out what to do about the swarming zombies. "How are you guys doing out there?" Ashley asks.

"We're holding our own for now, but they're sure trying to swarm us," James replies.

"I can't get over how many of them there are," Brad stammers.

"Well, it's obvious we can't kill them all," Chad finally admits.

"They're going to kill us all," Brad says in a strangled voice.

"Not if I have anything to say about it," declares James.

"We need to come up with an escape plan," suggests Ashley.

"The ship is the only sure way to escape, but we have to get to it first," says James.

"Brad and I have the robots," continues James. "We can clear a path for Ash and Chad to get to the ship. Chad, you need to get the ship running."

"I'm not leaving here without you," Ashley says to James, "and I'm not leaving Brad behind, either."

"If we all try to make a break for the ship, they're just going to swarm the ship," James points out to her. "Once you two are on the ship and have it running, Brad and I will get to the ship."

"What if you can't?" Ashley says, giving voice to her most terrifying thought. "There's a lot of zombies out there."

"I will do my absolute best to get Brad and I to the ship," James reassures her, "but if it's not enough, we'll have to cross that bridge when we get to it."

Ashley relents but thinks to herself, "I'll die before I leave here without him."

Ashley reluctantly agrees to the plan, and Chad says, "I need some firepower if we're going to make the ship." He begins attaching a shotgun to a backpack hopper preparing to assist in their breakout. When they are all set to go, James instructs them to exit through the rear doors as it will be the shortest distance to the ship.

Ashley and Chad comply, and as they exit the rear doors, they are immediately met by a mob of zombies. "Don't stop whatever you do," Chad says to Ashley as he instantly starts shooting at the zombies trying to clear a path. James, still in Ashley's robot comes and helps clear a path to the boat for them, leaving Brad alone to deal with the majority of the swarm of zombies.

"Ok, you two—you've got some room, get going," James says as he drops enough zombies to clear the path to the ship. He continues advancing slowly, still firing on the zombies, soaking the ground and the surrounding zombies in blood and brain matter.

"Be safe," Ashley admonishes James before she hurries off.

Ashley and Chad race to complete the longest hundred-meter dash of their lives. Upon completing it, they finally reach the ship. Ashley immediately heads to the cabin to start the ship. "Wasn't I supposed to get it started," whines Chad.

"Just stay there and help him hold off the zombies while I get it done," Ashley retorts.

Chad and James continue firing to hold the zombies off. Once the ship jumps to life James suddenly veers off in an attempt to lure the zombies away from the ship. As James tries to lead the zombies away and Chad fires at the remaining ones keeping them from advancing on the ship, Ashley quickly releases the lines holding the ship to the dock and then returns to the cabin to keep the ship in place.

As James runs the majority of the zombies turn to give chase, Chad remains to fire at the remaining group of zombies keeping them from gaining access to the ship. Brad is now almost out of ammo, and he joins James in keeping the zombies' attention as they head for some oil barrels. Now that they have most of the zombies' attention, it is time to get on the ship.

As they reach the barrels of oil, they jump up and let the zombies swarm below them. As the swarm presses in getting closer and closer, they fire beneath them causing a massive explosion and burning the swarm. They strip out of their VR gear and grab the shotguns and sacks of ammo that Ashley and Chad had prepared for them before their exit from the warehouse.

Exiting the rear door, they are immediately set upon by some remaining zombies, and as they run for the ship, they shoot at them to keep from being overtaken. The gunshots attract the attention of some of the other zombies who instantly start sprinting at the two running humans. James and Brad continue shooting as they are running for their lives.

"You've got to hurry up Brad, we need to beat them to the ship," James calls out. Brad is doing his best, but he is not a physically active person and is not as fast as James. All the noise from the gunshots has attracted a small horde to them, and as they draw near the ship, the horde begins closing in. James jumps to the ship without breaking stride, but Brad is approaching with his back to the ship and will need to turn in order to jump.

James, landing safely on the ship, immediately turns and begins firing at the zombies to hold them back. As Brad turns and takes a few running steps to jump to the ship one of the zombies launches itself out of the horde and tackles him to the ground. Ignoring the searing pain in his side, Brad looks at the ship and sees James still firing at the zombies and Chad gaping open-mouthed at him as he slips into blackness, his last thought is at least they got away.

 Ashley, heartsick at the lack of opportunities, must pull away as the zombies take her friend to prevent them from being able to jump aboard the ship. Chad falls to his knees, suddenly realizing the futility of trying to kill all the zombies. He begins sobbing as he realizes Brad's demise was all his fault. He was so focused on his revenge to the point that he wouldn't listen when warned of the dangers. He is distraught, as he sits there sobbing.

CHAPTER 11

With tears filling her eyes, Ashley throttles up the ship and heads out to sea. James joins her in the cabin shortly afterward. Not sure of what to say, he simply asks, "How are you making out?"

"I have no idea what I'm doing, or where we're heading," she says through her tears.

"Let's try some of these switches and levers and see what they do," James suggests.

Chad is still kneeling where James left him, sobbing as he watches the scene of his friend's demise slowly fade away into the distance. "I wish James had gotten pissed at me and just thrown me off," he thinks to himself. "I could have waded back and let the zombies eat me, too." He is overcome with grief and anguish. He never imagined that it would turn out this way.

As the grief settles in his gut and begins to turn to guilt, Chad slowly gets his sobbing under control. The grief keeps building on itself, while Chad sits sniffling wiping his face with his shirt sleeve. Suddenly, he bolts to his feet and lurches his way to the railing. Grasping the rail with both hands, he begins retching violently over the side of the ship.

"I have no clue where we're going," Ashley says to James.

"We need to figure it out, but all we have is a map and a compass," James agrees.

James takes the map over to the table at the side of the cabin and begins studying it. After a few minutes, he straightens and consults the compass.

Grunting to himself he heads back to the steering wheel and makes a few adjustments, consulting the compass until he announces, "We are on the right course now. I'm not going to bother with the rest of the switches. I don't want to mess anything up."

"No, let's just leave everything like it is," Ashley agrees.

They fall silent, both lost in their thoughts and dealing with the unexpected traumatic ending to Brad's life at the port before they got away. "I can't believe Chad couldn't see that starting the fires would lead to this," Ashley thinks to herself.

James thinks, "I tried over and over again to warn him, but he wouldn't listen."

Chad, finished being sick, wipes his mouth on his sleeve and stumbles back to where he dropped the shotgun. Bending over, he retrieves it before standing while weaving as he looks around the ship. Spotting what he thinks is a stairway he stumbles off in search of somewhere to be alone with his guilt.

Unsteady on his feet, he then manages to gain the stairway and, descending into the bottom of the ship, he trips and falls down the last few steps. As his head contacts the floor, his last thought is, "Damn it! I can't even walk anymore." Then, he sinks into unconsciousness, relieved for the moment from the burden of guilt.

"I've never driven a ship before," James says to Ashley. "I have no clue what I'm doing."

"Well, as my dad used to tell me when I was in school," Ashley says, "Just fake it till you make it!"

James can't help but to laugh and is surprised when even with all the tension and devastating emotions surrounding Brad's death, he feels a little lighter.

Thoughts of Brad automatically cause his thoughts to turn to Chad. "He was certainly taking Brad's death hard the last time I saw him," James thinks to himself. "I'll have to check on him later," he promises himself. Wrenching his mind back to the task at hand, James turns back to the control panel.

James looks at the gauge that shows their speed and checks the compass again to ensure they are still on course. Turning to the map, he grabs up a pencil and a scrap of paper and begins jotting down numbers.

"What are you doing?" Ashley inquires.

"I'm calculating the speed and direction we're traveling so that I'll know when we need to turn back towards land to reach Hakodate," James explains.

"That way if our speed and direction remain the same, all we need to do is check the time," Ashley says.

"Exactly. Without having the navigational equipment—and not knowing how to use it anyway—this should make do," James replies. "I just want to double-check my calculations to make sure they're right," James says as he turns back to the table with his paper on it.

Satisfied that his calculations are accurate, James turns to Ashley and says, "I'm sorry Brad didn't make it to the ship. Maybe I should have stayed behind him and let him get on first."

Ashley steps to James and wraps her arms around him and, laying her head on his shoulder, says, "I'm sorry he didn't make it, too, but if you had stayed behind, the zombies would have gotten you and maybe him, too. It may sound selfish—and if it does, I'm sorry—but as much as I miss Brad and wish he had made it, I'm not sorry that you did, and I wouldn't have been willing to trade you for him."

James' arms come up around Ashley and hold her close. He can't believe how much she has come to matter to him in such a short time. "I wouldn't have let you be taken even if it meant my life," he whispers against Ashley's hair. Inhaling the scent of her everything in him settles. He is baffled at how this can happen but enjoys it just the same. "Thank you," he whispers.

Pulling apart their conversation turns to Chad. "I didn't realize that he and Brad had grown so close," Ashley says.

"Were they that close?" James asks.

"From the way that he's taking it they must have been somewhat close," Ashley responds.

"I wasn't sure if his reaction was because they were close or because he felt guilty," James admits.

"I think it must be a combination of both," Ashley says.

Chad stirs as consciousness returns and briefly wonders why he is laying on the floor. Memory comes smashing in bringing with it all the grief and guilt he had been carrying since Brad was taken by the zombies. He really hates the zombies now, but the knowledge that they can't kill them all is devastating to him.

Pulling himself up off the floor he retrieves the shotgun from where it had gone sliding when he fell. Looking both right and left, he decides to go towards the rear of the ship so as to be furthest away from Ashley and James, who he assumes will still be up in the cabin directing the ship.

"Chad does seem to have developed quite a bond with Brad," James says a few minutes later.

"I didn't think he was capable of that much feeling," Ashley reflects on the interactions she has been part of or witness to since meeting at the warehouse. It's hard for her to mesh the two sides of Chad she has witnessed.

"I wonder what he went through before he came to the warehouse," Ashley says, more thinking out loud than talking. "He sure did seem to be taking it hard when we left the port," Ashley agrees.

"I wonder if talking about it would help him or only make it worse," James ponders out loud.

"It's hard to say," Ashley says. "Different people deal with things in different ways."

"It might not hurt to try, I guess," James says.

"I better check our course again," James says as he moves away from Ashley to consult the compass. Ashley moves over to watch what James is doing and to make sure she knows what setting the compass needs to be on.

"So as long as this needle is pointing right here," Ashley says, motioning to the compass, "we will be going in the right direction."

"That's right," responds James.

Chad stumbles along until he finds himself in a dark room at the rear of the ship. Looking around he notices more stairs leading up to the deck from this room. He briefly wonders if there would be stairs at the front of the ship too. Then spotting a chair in the corner of the room he stumbles over to it and flops down. The scene of Brad's demise keeps playing over and over in his head as he wonders what he could have done differently besides not starting the fires in the first place.

He is in such a state that he has to admit to himself that James and Ashley both tried to warn him of this—how he wishes now that he had listened to them. Unable to go back and change anything, he realizes he will just have to live with the fact that he killed the best friend he had ever known. He's not entirely sure how he is supposed to do that.

"Chad sure seemed to be taking it hard when we left," James muses. "He just buckled to the floor and started sobbing."

"I felt so bad for him, but I didn't know what to do."

"I could hear him wailing all the way up here," Ashley agrees. "I hope he's going to be ok."

"I don't know if he has any experience dealing with this kind of traumatic loss. Do you?" James asks.

"I don't know. He never really said what happened before he came to the warehouse—just that he had been heading that way for days," Ashley reports.

"Well, from the amount of hatred he had for the zombies and how badly he wanted revenge on them," James says as a matter of fact, "we have to assume he had at least some sort of loss associated with the appearance of the zombies."

"Yes, that is probably a safe assumption," Ashley admits, "but that means he is familiar with trauma—but it could also mean he has already endured as much as he can."

"This then means that he could be close to the edge," sighs James.

James is worried about Chad, from just the little bit he said at the port, he knows he is blaming himself, and that is a lot of guilt to carry around. Coupled with the fact that Chad isn't known for making the most intelligent decisions he is extremely worried for him. Ashley sensing the turbulent thoughts tossing around in James lays her hand on his back and softly says, "If you're worried about him and want to go check on him, I can stay here and monitor our course."

"You sure that you wouldn't mind?" James asks her.

"Not at all," Ashley replies. "We don't have to change course until three o'clock," James tells her.

 "Thank you, Ashley. I just need to make sure he's ok," James says as he exits the cabin.

Chad is sinking deeper and deeper into despair. He doesn't know how to deal with the anguish he feels not to mention the guilt. If I hadn't pushed so hard to kill all the zombies to be able to stay in Tokyo, Brad would be alive now, he thinks to himself. Unable to sit still Chad decides to get up and wander the ship for a while—thinking that keeping his mind busy studying the ship may bring some level of relief.

James exits the cabin, turning to look back at Ashley as he heads to the entrance where he had left Chad when they left the port. Walking into the entrance area, James looks around and can't find Chad anywhere. He is torn between continuing to look for him and letting Ashley know that he has to look for him first. Deciding she can keep a lookout in case, she sees him. First, he traces his steps back to the cabin.

Chad works his way towards the front of the ship, studying every room thoroughly and committing every detail he can to memory along the way. It is an effort to occupy his mind on things other than Brad's death. That is how he coped with it when mere hours after the appearance of the chemical cloud that created the zombies his parents were eaten by the zombies trying to save him.

He wishes now, even as he knows it would never have happened that his parents had just saved themselves. "They would never have caused their best friends deaths," he thinks to himself. He is beginning to develop a severe case of self-loathing. Trying desperately to distract his mind he begins running his hands over the intricate carving in some of the trim work trying to memorize the details.

Ashley is surprised when James returns to the cabin so quickly, and one look at her face tells her he is more concerned than when he left. "He's not where I left him," James says in a drawn voice. "I just thought I'd let you know so you can keep an eye out for him, too, if he happens to come up this way."

"If he happens to come here, I'll talk to him," Ashley says, "and if I see him up that way, I'll use the intercom to let you know."

"Thanks, Ash," James whispers while his lips are descending to hers for a brief kiss before heading out to search the ship for Chad.

Chad is nearing the front of the ship, and it almost seems as with every step his despair grows increasingly larger. As hard as he tries he can't keep his mind from focusing on the happenings of the day. It is as if it is on a never-ending loop in his mind. I can't deal with this much longer he thinks to himself. Then he pauses seeming just to realize he is still carrying the shotgun with him. After a few moments pause, he continues on to the front of the ship, no longer investigating as he goes.

CHAPTER 12

James decides to search the back of the ship on the deck before descending to the lower level. He checks every room as he makes his way to the back. As he is searching the ship for Chad, he has plenty of time to think. He thinks back over all the interactions he had with Chad and Brad at the warehouse while they were there. He begins to wonder if he should have tried to get Brad and Chad to switch places operating the robot but decides that wouldn't have worked either.

Deciding that there was no way of predicting that Brad wouldn't make it to the ship, James consoles himself with the fact that three of them survived the attack by the zombies— having decided that, his mind shifts to Chad's well-being. He is very concerned about Chad's state of mind right now.

As he reaches the rear of the ship, he descends the stairs and looking around finds himself in a dark room. As his eyes adjust, he spots the chair in the corner of the room and walking over to it, he realizes the floor is covered in dust, and he can see Chad's footprints where he had walked to the chair, and where he had left from the chair.

Chad had decided that they are better off without him and that he can't live with the guilt of having caused his best friend to die. Mingled with the guilt is the fact that he had never even let Brad know that he was his best friend. Now he would never have the chance. Not in this life at least.

James starts out checking all the rooms he comes to until he realizes he's following Chad's footprints into and out of the rooms. He then decides it would be better just to follow his footprints. This makes his search progress much faster. He comes to the stairs in the center of the ship and sees what looks like where Chad had fallen down.

Chad reaches the stairs at the front of the ship and pauses with one foot on the bottom step. He wants to make sure he is making the best decision before he follows through with it. He wishes with everything in him that he could change the situation he is in, but knowing he can't go back, he decides the only thing left is to move forward with his plan.

Ashley knows that everyone is upset but that they should really eat. She decides to talk it over with James when he gets back. She is hoping the people at Hakodate are still there and doing ok. She wishes that Chad and Brad had just agreed to come with them without trying to set the city on fire first. They could have had everything loaded on the ship and had the guys operate the robots from the ship. Then, nobody would have had to make it to the ship—they would have *already* been on the ship.

James studies the marks on the floor—and then turning to look at the steps, he notices the bottom three steps and the hand railings in the same area are still covered in undisturbed dust. Judging from the marks he sees, James thinks it is safe to assume that Chad must have tripped and fallen down the last three stairs. Seeing the blood on the floor in the dust, he wonders how badly Chad was hurt in the fall.

As Ashley checks the readings on the compass, their speed and the time again she is still worrying about James and Chad and wondering what they will find when they get where they're going. Suddenly out of the corner of her eye she spots Chad coming up the stairs from the lower level and heading to the bow of the ship.

As James finishes making his diagnosis of what happened with Chad at the stairs, he begins following his footsteps towards the front of the ship. Noticing they are going in and out of every room still, he stops and ponders what Chad had been doing checking each room. The thought occurs to him that he may have been trying to divert his mind from the tragedy just as the intercom crackles.

Ashley, figuring out how it works, activates the intercom and alerts James that Chad is at the bow of the ship near the railing. Knowing that James has no way to communicate with her and let her know he heard her, she knows she will just have to wait and see if he shows up before repeating the message again.

She is hoping Chad had been too absorbed in his thoughts or maybe too near the water to have been able to hear the message. She doesn't want him to know they are looking for him and decide to bolt. Not like he could go far she thinks as she notices James coming up the stairs.

After hearing Ashley's message, James had given up following Chad's footprints but had still noticed when they stopped going in and out of each room. This makes him think Chad has decided on a plan and he doubts it's a good one. Ascending the stairs, he spies James at the railing in the bow of the ship and heads in his direction.

Chad grasps the railing and leans over looking at the water passing beneath the ship. He wonders what it would be like to just flop over the railing and sink beneath the waves. He figures that with his luck, the ship wouldn't hit him and knock him out, and it would be too long and painful a death. Probably nothing more than I deserve he thinks, but still not what he wants to endure.

As he straightens up, he suddenly becomes aware of footsteps approaching from behind. Swinging around and bringing the shotgun up in front of him he sees James approaching and yells at him, "Don't come any closer." Chad steps up onto the bottom rail behind him.

James raises his voice slightly as he calls out to Chad, "Calm down, I'm here to help you." I didn't realize he was this close to a foolish act of desperation, James thinks to himself. This is going to be harder than I thought.

"I don't need your help, and I don't want it," Chad screams back at him, clutching the shotgun tightly to himself as if he expects James to try and rip it from his grasp.

"I know you're hurting Chad, and I understand that you're devastated about what happened to Brad, but it wasn't your fault," James says trying to get through to someone he's not sure wants to be gotten through to.

"It's my fault," blurts Chad bursting into tears. "He was the best friend I ever had, even if we hadn't known each other long and because of what I did, he's dead." Chad's voice raises to a shout by the end of his outburst. Ashley can see them through the window in the cabin, but she can't hear what they're saying. She's pretty sure they're arguing though.

"Sure, we could have done things differently," James says trying to share the blame, "but there was no way to know how it would end."

"You told me," Chad yells, pointing his finger at James, "that if I tried to burn the city, it would drive the zombies to us—and when you told us to come back to the warehouse, I kept trying to reach the gas station," Chad's voice trails off.

"Chad, people are only human, we make mistakes," James pleads with him, "but the important thing is to learn from our mistakes."

Chad looks thoughtfully at James for a moment before replying, "I am learning from my mistake. I'm learning that you two are better off without me."

James counters with, "That is so untrue, Chad. You were an instrumental part of us surviving at the warehouse." James is trying to keep Chad focused on the conversation as he slowly inches closer.

Ashley is watching the two guys through the window while still monitoring their direction and speed. She notices James slowly inching forward and correctly interprets his intentions to get close enough to grab the shotgun. She hopes he can be successful without getting himself hurt or worse.

"I was also the only person responsible for Brad dying," Chad shouts at James. James inches a few steps closer as he replies.

"No, Chad, you can't claim that. You may have started the fires, but Brad helped you. By the time we got back to the warehouse, Ashley and I were trying just as hard as you to help make sure everyone survived. So it's not all on you."

"That's all after the fact," Chad screams at him.

"After the fact of setting the fires, but the fires didn't kill Brad. All the gunshots Brad and I shot off attracted a lot more zombies to the warehouse than the fires had chased there," James points out shuffling a little closer. Brad pauses looking at James, trying to judge if he's just saying these things or if he really means it.

Ashley continues to monitor the gauges and compass, but she can hardly tear her eyes away from the view out the window. She notices James is close enough to grab the shotgun if he lunged for it but hopes he won't do that, because if Chad resists it could end up with someone getting shot and she doesn't want that someone to be James.

"It still doesn't change the fact that lighting the fires is what chased the zombies there, to begin with," Chad argues setting his jaw. James sees the set of Chad's jaw and realizes his task just got harder. He contemplated giving in, he thinks, but now he's stiffened his resolve.

"Chad, looking back in hindsight, it's easy to see ways that we could have done it differently," James says softly. "Like, if I hadn't been so pigheaded and had entertained your idea more, you wouldn't have had to go off and do it on your own." James is hoping Chad will see that it was a series of bad choices that caused the mission to fail as it did. That would alleviate some of his guilt.

Chad says, "You can't use that line on me. I was the one who chose to go ahead on my own." Then, noticing that while they're talking, James has moved to with fifteen feet of him, he continues, "I told you not to get any closer, James."

"I'm just talking to you, Chad," James replies to him. "All I'm saying," James continues, "is that there were a lot of bad choices that led up to what happened. And they weren't all made by you. That means you're not solely responsible for what happened."

"But you tried to talk me out of it," Chad says trying to use James' own argument against him. "That relieves you of any responsibility—that means it's all mine."

"You forget that Brad chose to go along with you, and he lit just as much of the fire as you did," James says to him, inching a few steps closer.

Ashley, watching through the window while she continues to monitor the compass and speed, thinks to herself, I think he's making progress. I think he's going to talk Chad into coming down off the rail. Maybe this will still end without anyone else getting hurt.

Chad pauses at this statement and seems to be thinking about it for a minute, and then he responds with, "You can try all the arguments in the world you want James, but you're not going to change my mind. You two are better off without me around."

"I disagree, Chad," James replies vehemently, "but even if that's so, when we get to Hakodate you don't have to stick with us."

"Those people don't need someone like me coming in to ruin their colony, either," Chad protests irately.

Ashley sees things heating up again and thinks Oh no, easy James, you've got to talk him down from there. "Come on, Chad!" James pleads with him. "Why don't you at least talk to us first and see if it helps. If that doesn't work, you can still carry on with your plan."

"Nice try," retorts Chad. "I give you my shotgun, and you'll hide it so I can't go through with my plan."

Realizing he needs to get the shotgun away from Chad, James inches forward another step. Chad notices the movement and thinks to himself, "I am so done with this. I can't let him get any closer, and I have no desire or intention to hurt him." Leaning back as James begins to inch forward another step,

Chad suddenly puts the shotgun barrel under his chin and pulls the trigger.

His head is obliterated in a spray of blood, bone and brain matter. Before James can scream, his headless body topples over the rail still clutching the shotgun in suddenly lifeless hands. James slowly sinks to his knees and brings his hands up to cover his face. As James begins to sob, Ashley, with tears streaming down her cheeks, quickly checks the settings again before bolting from the cabin and running to James.

She drops to her knees beside him and facing him wraps her arms around his shoulders pulling him close and letting him sob on her shoulder. James lays his head on Ashley's shoulder and grumbles, "Why couldn't I make him see?"

"Shush," Ashley shushes him. "You did your best. I sure hope this is the last friend we have to lose for a long time."

James and Ashley kneel there for a long time, holding each other and sobbing out the grief over the loss of their friend—as the boat drifts on towards Hakodate, unassisted but miraculously maintaining course.

CHAPTER 13

After what seems like forever kneeling and holding onto each other, James and Ashley rise and slowly make their way back to the cabin. As they come through the door, Ashley releases James' hand—and sinking into the chair off to the side of the room, she draws up her knees and wraps her arms around her legs before lowering her head to rest on her knees.

James pushes through the fog in his brain and, after a few false starts, manages to check the compass and speed indicator and checks the time. Seeing that they are still on course and have a while left before needing to turn, he slowly shuffles his way across the cabin feeling like the weight of the world is on his shoulders. Pulling up a chair, he flops down beside Ashley and gently rubs his hand up and down her back as she sits there silently sobbing.

"I am very sorry. I couldn't talk him down from the railing," James says.

Ashley raises her head and turns to look at James with tears streaming down her cheeks and replies, "Oh, I don't blame you, James—not at all. I hate all this death, and it hurts, but I'm glad you didn't get hurt trying to save him."

"I think he had his mind made up about the outcome before he even reached the bow, never mind me talking to him," James stammers through the sobs gradually slowing down.

Ashley vaguely recalls that before Chad shot himself, she had been planning to discuss the option of eating with James. She can feel her stomach rumbling, but with the recent trauma of watching Chad blow his head off, she has no desire to eat at all. "I could use something to drink, though," she thinks to herself.

Turning to face James and running her hand gently over his folded hands until he looks up at her through bleary eyes filled with sorrow, she asks James, "Where did our food and supplies get put?"

James looks at her and blinks—a faraway look coming into his eyes as he tries to recall that far back past the latest tragedy. Suddenly, his eyes come into focus, and he says, "I hate to tell you, Ash, but we have no supplies. Chad threw them at the zombies, trying to distract them when Brad and I were dashing for the ship. I'm so sorry, Ash," James says as he hangs his head.

"So you mean we have to make it all the way to Hakodate with no supplies?" Ashley asks him.

"I'm afraid so, Ash," James replies.

With a sad smile, Ashley turns to James and says, "At least, we don't have to worry about who's going to do the cooking."

James can't even manage a chuckle at Ashley's attempt at humor, but he does at least find the strength to muster a grimace. "Some ships have a system for converting sea water to potable water," James says to Ashley, "but I have checked all the switches, and I have no idea if this one has one—or how it works even if it does."

They fall silent as they each drift into their own thoughts. Ashley thinks that this whole trip would have been a lot more jovial without the loss of not one but two of their friends. Granted they hadn't known each other long, but living in the conditions they had been living in everything seems to have been sped up, relationships developed quicker and grew deeper way faster than they would have in the time before the appearance of the zombies.

Her thoughts return to that morning in the ship before the first explosion alerted them to Chad and Brad's doomed attempt at trying to burn the city and kill all the zombies. She remembers James starting to lift her shirt, and admits she was hoping, when the explosion interrupted, that during the trip they could find the time and privacy to continue.

James' thoughts are running along a similar line, and he can almost feel the hem of Ashley's shirt grasped in his hand as he raises it off her body—allowing his eyes the first glimpse of her with only her bra on. He blinks his eyes unable to believe how real it seems until Ashley kisses him, and he realizes he's not dreaming. His hands working of their own accord have removed Ashley's shirt, and he is feasting on the sight of her.

He looks down at the shirt grasped tightly in his fist and raising his eyes to Ashley's notices the love streaming out of her eyes, even as the sorrow is receding to the side, unable to stand in the face of the love shining from her eyes. "Is this wrong or disrespectful?" James whispers to Ashley, not wanting to break the spell he feels weaving around them, dissipating—if only for a brief interlude—the racking pain and grief that they have been feeling.

"No, James," Ashley replies with feeling, "This is not wrong, nor is it disrespectful. Just as relationships develop quicker in the time that we're living in. Life is so perilous; grieving has to be shortened as well." James raises his lips to Ashley's and slowly succumbs to the heat coursing through his veins as they undress each other and gently lower each other to the floor of the cabin.

Ashley is burning with desire for James, and if she's honest with herself, she has been for a long time. She is sorry it has to come on the heels of so much trauma and hurt, but now it can act as a healing salve as well as strengthening their bond. She slowly loses all focus on anything but James and what they are doing to and with each other.

As they lay wrapped in each other's arms, the heat of passion spent, reality returns and brings with it the memories of all the traumatic events of the day. Ashley notices the grief and sorrow have returned, but not as strong as it was earlier. Turning to James, she softly says, "I think your love has alleviated some of the sorrow. There's still lots there that I don't know if I could deal with anymore, but it feels a little bit dull now."

James pulls her closer and places a soft kiss on her lips before replying, "I know what you mean; I feel it, too. I'm still devastated by what has happened, especially Chad, but it's been dulled." Reaching over to pick up his watch, James looks at the time and says, "I better get up and check our route; it's almost time to turn this ship to shore."

James gathers up his clothes and gets dressed then moves over to the table where the map and his calculations are. He checks the compass and their speed, and compares with the map, checking his calculations for the last leg of the journey. "I keep forgetting Chad is gone," James says to Ashley.

"I know what you mean," Ashley replies. "I was going to say it was good he didn't come to the door earlier." Ashley reddens and sighs.

"I can still see it's possible," James explains, "but then, when I'm in the middle of doing something, for a minute, I'll forget."

Ashley reaches for his hand and reassures him, "I'm sure as time goes by it will get easier. At least I hope it does." After pausing for a minute and licking her lips, she sinks into the chair and looking up at James asks, "Are you sure there's no water or anything to drink on this ship?"

"My stomach thinks my throat's been cut," Ashley says, "and my mouth feels like it's filled with sandpaper.

"I know it's been a long time since we've eaten or had anything to drink," James says. "I hope that there are people at Hakodate, or we might not make it, Ash."

"I had the same thought," Ashley whispers.

James looks at Ashley sitting on the chair, looking disheveled and worn out. Not nearly the strong, vibrant young woman he knows she is. Realizing the toll that the last couple of tragedies has had on her, James says, "I'm sorry for all the trauma we've had lately." Then, lowering his head slightly, he adds bashfully, "I'm also sorry our first time had to be on this dusty floor and not in a big soft bed."

Color rises up Ashley's cheeks, and she looks at James and replies, "I'm glad it came whether on a dusty floor or anywhere else; I wouldn't change it for anything." Pausing thoughtfully for a minute, she looks longingly at James and continues, "In fact, as traumatic and life-changing as the zombies have been and everything they've caused, I wouldn't change that either. That is what brought us together."

James is amazed at the feelings that flow through him as Ashley says this. He stares unblinkingly at Ashley as he thinks back over all the things the appearance of the zombies has cost him. He focuses on Ashley, and as a weak smile lifts his lips, he says, "Ashley, I could have lost twice as much as the appearance of the zombies cost me, and I wouldn't trade it for anything. I'm actually thankful for the zombies coming. That's what brought you to me."

James consults his figures and the compass before looking at his watch. He turns the ship until he gets it lined up on the new heading they need to reach Hakodate. It's not until he has the new course set and Ashley comes up beside him, laying her head on his shoulder that he looks out the window and realizes the fog is rolling in.

James shuffles across the floor—it's about the only method of moving he has the strength left for—and slumps down in the chair next to Ashley. Placing his hand gently on hers he revels in the warmth that radiates from their hands being joined. Turning to look at her he says, "We may have a hard time finding the dock where we're going," as he motions out the window.

Ashley turns and looks out the window for the first time since they had come into the cabin earlier. She is amazed by the thick billowy whitish fog that is rolling in, almost seeming to boil. "Is that ever thick?" she says to James. "How will we ever make it there in this?"

James smiles at her and replies, "We are navigating with the compass and the map, so we'll be ok getting there—until we need to see."

Ashley looks out the window again and then turns to look at James and says, "This must be what they're referring to when they say they are socked in."

"Yes, Ash," James agrees, "I think you are right. We are socked in." Looking lovingly at Ashley. James briefly squeezes her hand before saying, "I think I should go sit by the steering wheel, Ash. I'd like to stay here with you, but I don't have the strength to keep going back and forth."

"I can bring this chair up there and sit with you there," Ashley replies. "Let me bring it up there for you," James suggests. Ashley is touched by the offer of chivalry when he is already so worn out. Standing up, she slowly makes her way up to the steering wheel as James drags her chair up. Once Ashley is seated James leans against the window at the side of the cabin letting his strength recover a bit before going to retrieve the other chair.

James returns, dragging the other chair and reaching the control area. He scans the speed indicator and the compass and then reads the time off his watch. Looking out the window, he says, "I sure hope this clears up before we get close to land."

"Yeah," Ashley agrees, "it would sure make it easier to spot where we are going."

As they continue on their course, James takes to scanning out the windows frequently. He knows they are still a little way out from land, but he doesn't want the ship running into something because they can't see it. He figures the closer they get to land the higher the risks of that will be.

Noticing James checking out the windows more and more frequently Ashley asks, "Are you looking for something specific?"

James looks out the window scanning the area in front of the ship before turning to Ashley and replying, "Not for something specific—no. I'm mostly just checking on the fog, and trying to see ahead of us to make sure we don't run into something."

Ashley gets a playful smirk on her face and says, "Yeah, it would sure suck to go through all that and endure the journey with no food or drink just to drown cause we sunk the ship."

James is almost continuously scanning out the windows trying to pierce the rolling fog enough to see anything that might be ahead of them. Ashley is trying to peer through the fog as well. She doesn't want the responsibility to rest fully on James. "Do you think we're getting close?" she asks James.

James consults the compass and the speed dial and reading the time turns to the map. He glances at his figures a few times and back to the map. Then, he turns to Ashley and says, "I think we can probably slow it down a bit. We should be getting pretty close. I don't want to come on land too quickly and not be able to avoid something."

As James reaches to pull back on the throttle a bit, Ashley points out the window and says, "What is that?"

James looks out the window and can just make out a rock pointing up through the fog off to their left. "Guess it is a good time to slow it down."

CHAPTER 14

James eases the throttle back and stares out the window. He can just barely make out the land in the distance through the fog. He notices that near the edge of the water, the fog seems to thin out a bit and become more like a mist than the thick clouds of rolling fog that they had been staring at.

He throttles back, thus slowing their approach to the port that takes shape slowly out of the mist ahead. Ashley stands up beside him, looking out through the fog at the port house that slowly comes into sight. James can feel her hand tremble on his arm. He turns to Ashley and says, "It's ok, Ash, I'm nervous as well, but we'll be ok. I'm not even sure if we're in the right place or if there will be people here, but we'll manage."

Ashley simply squeezes his arm gently in response. As the port house becomes clearer, Ashley's grip on his arm then becomes much tighter. "That's just like the one we left in Tokyo," she says to James.

"Look at those spiked barricades protecting it," he says to Ashley. "If we had those in Tokyo, the zombies would never have gotten close to the house."

As they ease their way towards the dock in the port, James notices people coming out of the house. He points them out to Ashley and can feel her body relax as she lets out a pent-up breath. "At least, we know we won't be here alone," she says to James, "although some time alone with you would be heavenly."

As they feel the excitement rise from being able to see the port they had set out for without knowing what they would find, the excitement is mixed with relief. James eases the ship up to the dock, and he puts his arm around Ashley's waist. He helps her down from the ship. They stumble their way off the dock onto the land, and as they reach the solid ground, they both slump to the ground too weak to continue.

The survivors from the house rush down to them and, picking them up, carry them into the house. They set them down at a table and bring them some juice to drink, knowing that they are dehydrated and probably starving. They can see that the new arrivals are very haggard-looking and can only imagine what they had been through before getting here.

One of the women from the group of survivors warms up some soup for the newcomers. When it is ready, she brings two bowls and sets it down in front of them. Looking at them through friendly eyes, she says, "Eat up. It'll restore some of your strength." James looks at Ashley and, placing his hand possessively on her leg, begins to eat as she smiles at him and picks up her spoon.

The group of survivors that are at the port house move off into the living room to give the newcomers some space while they eat. The woman who had warmed up the soup for them comes in and sits down at the table with them. "I'm Jenny," she says simply, "and you are safe here."

Seeing the tears begin to well up in Ashley's eyes, Jenny is worried that she may have upset the newcomers—but as Ashley speaks, realization dawns. Jenny then smiles. Ashley is saying, "I'm Ashley, and this is my boyfriend, James. We are happy to be here. We heard you call for help and headed this way. These are tears of relief at finally being safe. We lost two of our friends—one as we were getting on the ship and the other on the way here."

"Thank you for bringing us in," James says. "I don't think I could have gotten us up here by myself."

"You're more than welcome," Jenny says. She turns and motions at one of the men sitting in the living room, who quickly gets up and moves to her side. "This is my husband, Jason," she says as an introduction.

Ashley responds, "It is nice to meet you, Jason. I am Ashley, and this is my boyfriend, James."

James leans across the table and shakes Jason's hand. He smiles his welcome at Jenny and, finishing his soup, says, "Thank you! That was so delicious." He picks up his juice and sips slowly at it.

"You are quite welcome," Jenny says as she gathers the dishes and takes them back to the kitchen.

James pulls up a chair at the table, and Jenny returns with a coffee pot and some cups. "Is that really coffee?" James asks in awe.

"It sure is," Jenny says with a smile. "Oh, I haven't drank coffee in so long," James moans.

Jenny pours them coffee and, setting the pot on a coaster, she returns to the kitchen for fixings and comes back to sit down with the newcomers. "We'll have our coffee and then let you get a shower and some rest," Jason says to them. "We have an underground bunker just a short trip away from here," he explains. "It is left over from WWII, and we have mostly eliminated the zombies now. You're finally safe. After you have some time to recuperate from your experience, we'll find a place where you fit in, and you can help out. You're welcome to remain and be part of our little colony of survivors."

"If you're done with your coffee, Ashley, I can take you to the shower and let you get cleaned up," Jenny offers. Rising, Ashley gives James a gentle kiss before heading off with Jenny to the shower. While Ashley is in the shower, Jenny looks through the clothes that they have in the house and finds some clothes that she is sure will fit Ashley. "Just putting some clothes in here for you," Jenny says to Ashley as she opens the door and laying the clothes on the counter quickly exits.

"Would you like some more coffee?" Jason offers, reaching for the pot.

"Oh yes, please," James eagerly responds. Jason chuckles as he refills James' cup. As James adds fixings to his coffee, Jenny returns and sits down beside Jason. James begins to tell them their story—starting with their meeting at the warehouse.

With pride in his voice, he tells about Ashley building her own super robot out of extra parts. He gets to the part where they had just finished loading the stuff on the ship, and his mind is wandering over his brief time with Ashley before the explosion.

Jenny, correctly reading the expression on his face, says, "You and your girlfriend got a little alone time, then?"

"Almost," says James. "It would have been our first, but then there was an explosion." Jenny is surprised that James and Ashley's relationship is so new but says nothing.

James continues on with his story explaining about trying to set the city on fire by blowing up the gas stations and ending up accomplishing nothing but chasing the zombies right to their home. As he explains how he sent Ashley and Chad to the ship and him and Brad tried to lead the zombies off, everyone is impressed.

When he gets to the part about Brad not being able to make it on the ship, a silence descends on them. They are all still sitting there when Ashley walks in from her shower. "Wow, you look great," James exclaims as she walks in, dressed in the new clothes Jenny had brought for her.

"Thank you," she says to James. Turning to Jenny, she says, "Thank you, too, for the new clothes. I feel much better."

"No problem at all," Jenny assures her as Ashley sits down beside James.

"Why don't you get Ashley some more coffee if she wants some, hon?" Jenny says to Jason. "Meanwhile, I'll go show James to the shower." James stands and places a soft kid on top of Ashley's head as he turns and follows Jenny to the shower, thinking how nice it feels to be free of the threat of the zombies.

The mutated zombie steals stealthily across the ground, keeping low to reduce the likelihood of being seen. He is certain that the gate leading to the compound from the path to the sea was left unlocked when they carried the new survivors in. Dodging from cover to cover he approaches to within ten feet of the gate.

Motioning to his fellow zombies he watches them steal their way to position within thirty feet of him. Now all he has to do is get through that gate and find cover without being spotted. Scanning for cover to head to he notices the back wall of the house has no windows at this end.

When James returns from the shower he enjoys another coffee

before Jenny leads him and Ashley to a bedroom at the front of the house to get some rest. As he gets ready for a nap he suddenly whips around to look out the window. "What is it", Ashley asks. James is studying the landscape out the window. "I thought I saw something out there, just habit I guess. I'm not used to being safe yet." Ashley laughing replies, "Yeah, it's not like the zombies are smart and do a strategic attack."

Jason turns to Jenny and says, "I have an uneasy feeling. I keep looking outside expecting to see a horde of zombies coming." Jenny pats his hand and says, "Relax, we're safe. They can't get past the fence and our lookouts haven't spotted any zombie hordes in weeks." Jason lets out a deep sigh and says, "I know. That's what's bothering me. They've only seen about three or four individual zombies." "What's wrong with that", Jenny asks. "Zombie's don't usually wander around alone", Jason replies.

The leader of the mutated zombies inches closer and easing open the latch, he silently swings open the gate. Motioning to the rest of the crew to follow he duck walks to the back side of the house and waits for the rest to join him. As the last one comes through the gate he takes the time to silently swing the gate shut but leaves the latch undone.

Jason, still feeling uneasy walks around the house checking the view out all the windows. "I don't know why, but I can't shake this uneasy feeling", he says to the couple seated in the living room. "You just need to relax", one of them replies to him, "You're not used to being safe. We haven't seen any zombies in weeks."

As Jason completes his rounds, James emerges from the room. "How did you sleep", Jason says in greeting. "Restless, I just can't shake this uneasy feeling", James replies. Jason stops and looks at him, and says, "You know, we haven't seen any zombies in three weeks, but I have an uneasy feeling too." "Do you think they could develop intelligence, ability to communicate or plan", James asks.

As they turn and head to the kitchen area Ashley emerges from the room and follows along behind. "I never thought of that", Jason says to James' earlier question. "I'm going to discuss that with our scouts and have them watch for unusual behavior in any zombies they see. If they do adapt, I want to know about it."

As they sit down to the table there is the sudden sound of glass breaking and the screeching of zombies as they attack from all sides simultaneously. The women scream, Jason says, "Oh, Shit", and lunges for a gun. James says, "I knew it", and catches the gun Jason throws to him. The couple from the living room scream and they all turn to see the zombies swarm through the window and start ripping them apart.

James starts shooting at them exploding zombie's heads and splattering blood and gore all over the walls. The blood is running across the floor, and James is furiously loading his gun as Jason scans the rest of the house watching for other access points and Jenny is on the radio to the WWII bunker calling for help

"They have us surrounded, and they're inside the compound. They're coming from all sides at once. We need help, and we need it now." Jenny replaces the radio and brings the guys more ammo. Ashley retrieves a gun for her and Jenny. Handing one to Jenny they all begin scanning the windows for zombies.

At the WWII bunker the first wave of the survivors defense team races to the aid of those under attack. As they approach the compound and start firing on the zombies, they are not prepared for the second wave of zombies that was waiting in ambush and rushes them with a screech like they have never heard, and never will again as the zombies attacking the house turn and they are swarmed from both sides.

James sees the attack from inside and says, "We were never the target, we were the bait." Jason says, "What do you mean", and James explains what he just saw. As he finishes Jenny grabs the radio and reports to the bunker. They ready their next wave of defense.

As the next wave comes running and the zombies start falling James is awed and stands still. The new defense is something he's never seen. The guns they are firing is actually their arm, and it spins as it shoots. Looking at their faces he notices they don't have eyes. They have what he has only seen in the movies and can only explain as cyborg vision. James wonders if they're still human, but is glad they're on his side whatever they are.

www.ingramcontent.com/pod-product-compliance
Lightning Source LLC
Chambersburg PA
CBHW060622310726
48982CB00003B/646